Room 39 takes us on a beautiful tour that highten... the beginning, calms our nerves immediately after, but glues our fingers to the rails until the end.

When you think that you can predict the outcome, she tells you, "Wait, there's more to explore."
And just when you feel evil has triumphed, then comes the good smiling back with the last laugh.

A well-crafted novel that will keep you in suspense till the last paragraph.
I ask, "how can one person write so well?"

When you think of a fictional thriller that takes you from the basest level of human exploitation to the basic expression of unconditional love among humans;
When you think of a perfect narration that explores individualism and the potency of togetherness;
When you want to read a book that contrasts unfettered evil and ethereal forgiveness; you just need to pick up this book and gulp down every line from start to finish.

ROOM 39

Cabiojinia

Room 39

A secret worth dying for;
A love worth killing for

The Heart Mender

ROOM 39

Contact Info

Website: cabiojinia.com

Email: cabiojiniaofficial@gmail.com

ISBN: 9798794016574

I'm grateful to God for the idea, strength, and discipline to finish this book.

I also thank all my blog readers for constantly pushing me to be a better writer and offer more value through my articles. Without your constant questions that showed your interest in Room 39, I wouldn't have done this.

And thanks to my lovely parents, whose support for me has remained immovable. Your prayers have been invaluable. God bless and keep you.

Vi voglio bene.

SIGN UP FOR MY NEWSLETTER

For daily inspirational articles, kindly sign up to my weekly newsletter on cabiojinia.com.

There are over 300 articles on the Gospel, **Personal Development, Leadership, Business, Education, Society & Lifestyle, Inspiring short stories, and Inspirational Nuggets.**

"Forgive us our debts as we forgive our debtors."
MATTHEW 6:12

ROOM 39

CONTENTS

ROOM 39

PART ONE

In the beginning

ROOM 39

CHAPTER 1

'Shut up young woman *abi* man! You're disturbing the serenity of this environment. What is wrong with you? Do you think that you're the only one interested in finding a way to leave this god-forsaken building? We've tried all your suggestions but none of them worked. Get out of that place before I spend the last ounce of strength in me to crack you down.' He barked.

'We all have families too; in case you were not aware. Nonsense!' He yelled.

'You see old man, were it not that I respect the few grey threads on that bald skull, I'd have smacked you like a child,' Chika retorted.

'I've been respectful all my life and worked hard to be where I am now, with people like you under me. So, you best believe that if I hear one more insult from you, I won't mind folding this garment of respect to deal with your old behind.' She thundered.

'And by the way, I'm a woman, a wife and a mother. Better watch it boy.' she concluded as she picked up her pen and continued to unravel the code.

A much-solicited silence suddenly walked into the room, with everyone gazing at each other as if waiting for the silence to speak.

Chika's response was completely new to everyone. No one had heard her speak with such anger in her voice. Although they hadn't known each other for long, seeing her snap back at Kachi was new and terrifying at the same time. Yes, she had every reason to even go farther.

That side of her had remained hidden. And it better remain hidden because they wouldn't want her to stop what she was doing. Her suggestions have been quite helpful to getting them to where they are now, although they haven't succeeded at their enterprise yet. No one wanted any rifts. Not now. Not even tomorrow, 'until we've gotten out of this place.'

After about five minutes, Ejike decided to dismiss the silence. He gently clears his dry throat and adorns a serious look as if he were a village chief that was invited to settle a dispute between two elders.

'Alright everyone, this isn't the time for needless disputes. It's not a time for any misogyny or disrespect. We're all in this together and the earlier we found a solution, the better for us.' He said.

The rest of the people gently nodded in agreement without uttering any words. Everyone wanted to conserve some energy for the work ahead. Their eyes were already growing dim and their throat dry for want of anything edible. Some even wondered how Kachi and Chika still had the strength to waste in unreasonable fights.

When Ejike was done with his exhortation, everyone returned to work.

***

Chika woke up at 4 am, quite early for her given that she starts work at 8 am, and her office is just seven minutes' drive from home. And in the worst-case scenario, it'll take her ten minutes to get to the office. She could even walk to the office if there is much traffic.

Her office is located on Pirro's Lane, named after the famous Mathematician, who, according to legend, was the legitimate son of Archimedes. Many people living in other parts of the state have questioned the authenticity of that story. But who cares, Pirro's lane was known for several other things even more attractive than being named after a Greek. It is both the political and intellectual hub of the region and housed the centre of power.

Chika knew it was going to be an important day in her career – a day she'll meet with the director of national intelligence to know if she'll be appointed to the prestigious post of the director of the Secret Service arm. She's worked with the agency for a little over a decade now.

Working in the force has been her dream as a child. She recalls how as a child she trained in martial arts while her mates did other sports. She loved the discipline, dedication, and determination.

She always enjoyed the stories her dad told her concerning his 'missions' in several parts of the world – the rigorous training sessions, sleepless nights, thought process, loneliness, but also the fightings and victories. All these triggered off some beautiful hormonal release in her each time she hears them. Like a neighbour once said when Chika was a toddler, 'She took the adrenaline of the father and the melatonin of the mother.' Maybe the percentage of adrenalin is more seeing the traits of Chika.

***

Chika's father, Dede, is a retired army general who was known around the neighbourhood. Dede, as he was fondly called by family, friends, and companions, never wanted his daughter to get into the armed forces.

He had not only seen wars, blood, sand, fire, and the rest, he had been in them, fought in them, led troops in them, lost friends, and colleagues in them, that he wasn't ready to allow his child to get into one.

Yes, he was excited telling the stories of his escapades, but he wanted them to remain stories and nothing more – just a variant of the fairy tales of the tortoise and the monkey that parents often tell their children. Maybe a bit extreme, but those were the stories he could remember, and his family didn't blame him for sharing them either.

His real name however wasn't Dede, but who cares. Everyone has gotten so used to calling him Dede that most of his friends don't even know his real name.

There's this funny story of when Chika was about getting into the university. She had picked up the form from a nearby post office and quickly filled it up. When she got to the counter to submit it, the postman checked and when he saw Dede written against the space for parent's name, he asked Chika 'Is that your father's name?' And Chika boldly said yes without blinking. The postman wasn't convinced but Chika insisted, and he had no option but to agree.

On her way home, she called her father to narrate how the entire process went.

'Can you believe the postman was questioning your real name? I mean, who is he to question my dad's name in the first place?' She began.

And Dede from the other end of the phone asked 'Nnem, and what did you tell him is my name?'

'I told him your name naah". Chika responded, showing how bad she felt when the postman asked.

'Which is?' Dede quizzed.

'Daddy, don't you know your real name again? Hmmm… I told him that your name is Dede. Or do you want me to tell lies?' She said with so much assurance. And Dede burst into loud laughter.

Well, Chika has always refuted this account of the event, but that hasn't stopped Dede from always telling the story each time he deems it necessary, which is… every time.

Just like he has never stopped joking about how he got several promotions in the military because of his deep, masculine voice that often cast some doubt on his real age. He always said that his superiors in the military respected his voice so much that he thinks that was the single most important factor that earned him multiple promotions. Anyway, Dede's ex-colleagues agree with him, so you can't argue much.

Dede's real name however was Uzoma, a name originating from the Eastern part of Nigeria, that means the good path or the good way.

***

So, Dede often sought ways to talk his daughter out of the idea of even becoming a police officer, let alone to become a military officer. Not because he felt that his beautiful daughter was incapable, but because she was the only child, and he desired to see her have a regular, normal family without the constant thoughts and fear of death on the battlefront.

Dede had lost his father to aortic stenosis – a heart disease – at the young age of 51 which almost got him into depression. The father had a bicuspid aortic valve, an inherited malformation where instead of three leaflets, the valve on the left side of his heart had two leaflets.

As the doctor would explain to him after his father's death, the presence of that defect, among others, predisposed the father to develop aortic stenosis – the narrowing of the opening of the aortic valve. That implied that his father's heart gradually became unable to pump sufficient blood from his heart to the other organs of the body. So, he'd often have symptoms like breathlessness, chest pain, fatigue, palpitations, and after a while, also the thickening of the ventricle (the heart chamber).

8

Dede's father was rushed to the hospital one evening after he fainted, losing consciousness. Upon getting to the emergency department, he was quickly taken to the operating room, but couldn't make it out alive. The doctor told him that had the symptoms been detected earlier and the malformation treated surgically, maybe he'd have stood a chance. But that was not to be because Dede was rarely at home, his mother was dead, and his younger brother was only ten years old at the time.

Dede was just 21 years old at the time of his father's death; he was on his first mission abroad for about a year.

'Had I been around,' he thought, 'maybe I'd have constrained him to visit the doctor more often than he did. Dad has always been a hardworking man but had this one defect - he took little or no care of himself. And after the death of mom, he worked so hard to train us.'

After the death of his father, Dede served for a few more years before coming home to settle down. He had paused his marriage to his childhood sweetheart because he didn't want to be far away from home; he wanted to be very close to his wife and to raise their kids together. So, after leaving the force, he took to commercial farming, engaging in livestock farming as well as starting a pineapple orchard.

He eventually married Nnenna, his childhood heartthrob from another state, but whose parents moved to Dede's state when Nnenna's father was asked to head the accounts department at the headquarters of one of the textile industries. They grew up loving one another before eventually deciding to spend the rest of their lives together as a couple.

So, coming from this heart-breaking experience of his father's death, Dede decided to always be close to his home until his children were married – he wanted to be there for them physically, spiritually, and materially.

Chika on the other hand maintained a burning desire to follow in the footprints of her father, or at least to become something similar. She was just so passionate about military strategies that she would stay up late studying the history of the great ancient empires and their war strategies – she ate every page on the Babylonian, Grecian and Roman empires, their army, and exploits.

As she grew up, and as the arguments over her future ambition ballooned, she became increasingly uncomfortable with her father's position and once attempted to leave the house. It took the intervention of her mother and neighbours to pacify her mind.

She eventually reached a middle ground with Dede – she was going to get done with college, and only after then pursue a military career if she was still interested. Her father agreed to this, praying that she meets someone on campus, maybe a male friend, who will talk her out of such "senseless" desire. Those prayers however went partially unanswered seeing where we are today.

***

So, Chika got up early this morning just like other times to get ready for work and to get her little son, Ebuka ready for school. At 4 am the alarm clock rang; she had gone to bed at 9:30pm with Ebuka, though he never wanted to because his favourite TV program was on air that night.

Ebuka was so interested in the show that he was willing to miss school the following day. 'This is serious!' Chika exclaimed within herself. Ebuka is never the type of child that dreads going to school, especially because of Miss Ifunanya, his Mathematics teacher whom he had grown to cherish.

On many occasions Ebuka has refused to go home immediately after school, preferring to stay a bit longer with her. So, for Ebuka to be reluctant, it must be for something much more appetising than her. Well, Chika had a special appointment the next day, so not even Ebuka's lovely TV program would make her a second late to it.

As the alarm clock rang, she calmly rolled over her ruffled but well-perfumed bedsheets to snooze it. Slowly she brought down her legs to the sides of the bed, tucks her feet into her slipas and stood up. As she walks towards the bathroom, stretching herself and releasing a few yawns, she realises that she only snoozed off the alarm and in 5 minutes it'll go off again. She quickly returns to turn it off altogether. The next one is set for 6 am when she'll wake Ebuka up.

In the bathroom, she quickly washed her mouth, washed her face, and headed back to the bedroom to pray. She knows that today's morning devotion with Ebuka would last for about ten to twenty minutes. So, she preferred pouring out her heart unto God for an hour before Ebuka gets up.

'Heavenly Father, I thank you for this morning. I'm so grateful for Your grace and strength in my life and my family. Thank You for the numerous blessings You've kept bringing our ways. I'm grateful for life and Your grace. Thank You for the success we had in our last antiterrorism operation'. Chika prayed. She goes on to pray for her son, invoking the protection and wisdom of God upon him. She also prays for her extended family, her fellow workers, and her Church.

Chika is what the Pentecostal Christians and evangelicals call a born-again child of God; she gave her life to Christ at age 19. Although she was raised in a Christian home, it wasn't until her university days that she had a personal encounter with the Lord and Saviour Jesus Christ.

***

One warm afternoon Chika was sitting under a tree shade getting some fresh air. She was done with her lectures for the day and wanted to spend some hours studying at the university library. The initial plan was to return to the students' lodge with her friend, get some rest before heading to the library to study. But on second thought, she decided to rest for some minutes under the shade instead.

12

Until this day, she still believes that it was God that planned everything.

While she sat on the bench, a young man came around, gently asking if he could share the bench with her. 'Of course, you can,' she replied, though she quietly prayed within her that the young man wouldn't make noise nor start a conversation; she was so exhausted. God answered her prayers, and the young man simply went on studying for about thirty minutes without saying a word, besides asking how she was doing when he arrived. A question to which she barely recalls if she answered or not.

After about thirty minutes, she was ready to go to the library for some studies.

'You had a good sleep, right?' he asked.

'Yes, I did. Thanks for not disturbing me.' She answered.

'Well, I should thank you because you allowed me to revise the last pages of my notes. I'm on my way to the exam hall. I had wanted to revise in the hall but there was so much noise that I decided to come apart in a quiet environment.' He said while glancing through the last equations on his notes.

'Alright dear, that means we both gained.' Chika replies looking at him. 'I'll be on my way to the library now, I have quite a lot to cover for my exams coming up next week.' She concluded.

'Ok, the library is a good place to study, especially when someone needs maximum concentration.' He adds.

Chika rises and heads to the library, while Ikenna finishes with his revision. They both exchange goodbye.

One of the days, Chika was invited by a female friend for a programme in her Church. At first, she didn't want to attend because of her health; she was feeling feverish. But after much persuasion by her friend, she decided to attend, believing that her smaller-than-a-mustard seed faith will be enough to attract God's healing upon her.

The church congregation was a mixed one; it spanned from children to people who were elderly, in their mid-80s. That day, the teaching from the Pastor centred on patience. There was something about the minister that got her so hooked and focused on him. There was something about the way he explained the Bible; it seemed quite easy to understand and very close to everyday life that she was amazed.

She was very excited after the Church service that she decided to pitch her tent there; she hasn't been regular with Church activities at school anyway. So, finding a place that stimulates her desire to know and serve God was a great discovery. Also, God answered her prayers and she felt better at the end of the service.

She asked her friend if she could join the sanitary department of the Church as she felt that she would do good in that area. It was on one of the occasions while serving in God's house that she discovered that Ikenna (also known as Ike) also frequented the same Church, serving in the media department. In months to come, they would talk more and eventually desire to spend the rest of their lives together.

The godly amorous relationship between Ike and Chika is one that developed over time. It wasn't the typical love at first sight because, at the time, both were fully immersed in their studies and service to God in the Church. In fact, before Chika began attending the Church, it was rumoured at some point that Ike was maritally involved with a sister from his faculty.

CHAPTER 2

After her prayers, Chika goes to have her shower and to get the breakfast ready for herself and her son. She also got ready some snacks that *Nnam* will eat while in school. *Nnam* or *Nna* is a fond name that Chika calls Ebuka. Although it translates as 'my father', it's an affectionate name that means 'my love, my darling' to Chika.

Ebuka's favourite snack is the egged fish, a name he coined for a snack that Ike, his father normally makes for him. It was an invention that Ike came up with during one of those lonely moments when he had nothing to eat in the university; a mixture of several things that normally wouldn't go together. Well, since he enjoyed the snack, who cares what everyone has to say, right?

After his wedding to Chika, one of the days, he decided to prepare for his lovely wife his bachelorhood favourite snack. Chika appreciated the effort and thought that went into the whole process but not the final product. But since she didn't want Ike to feel bad, she decided to modify the recipe a little… et voilà, the snack transformed into something more delicious… at least for Ike, and edible for Chika.

No one knew what name to give the snack all the while until Ebuka escaped the womb.

One of the holidays when they were taking a mini trip to the seaside, Ebuka asked, 'Daddy, are there egged fishes at the seaside?'

'Egged fish? Yes, darling. I think you'll see egged fishes there.' Ike replied, with a little wonder on his face as to what an egged fish means.

'Are they big and sweet to eat?' Ebuka continued.

'I think so, my dear. They should be big and sweet.'

'Have you eaten them before?' Ebuka quizzed further.

At this point, Ike didn't quite know what to answer. He had played along all the while pretending to know what Ebuka was talking about. But he no longer wanted to continue in the lies before he'd be caught. Chika on the other hand was just enjoying the dad-son conversation while giggling to herself; she knew that at some point Ike would be caught.

'Daddy, have you eaten the egged fish at the seaside before?' Ebuka insisted, seeing that his dad wasn't giving him any answers.

'Nnam, have you seen an egged fish before?' Ike responded.

'Yes, of course, Dad. I've seen it many times.'

'Ok my son, that's good. And how do they look?' Ike continued, winking at his wife who was sitting next to him.

'Well, they look like eggs. But Daddy, haven't you seen an egged fish before?' Ebuka quickly took over the questioning.

'Ehmm… ehmm… Nnam if you've seen it then I have seen it too, right?' Ike babbled.

'Yes, of course, Daddy. We always see and eat them together.' Ebuka insisted.

It was at this point that things began getting a bit curious. An innocent conversation was now turning into suspicion of several episodes of possible demonic possession in the dream or something.

'Where did he see these creatures? Who gave them to him? How was I there with him? Is anyone giving him something at school? Is this some demonic initiation in the dream using my face? What's happening?'

These and many more questions were going through the minds of Ike and Chika when the voice of Ebuka interrupted again. But this time, with an answer that pleasantly shocked them.

'Daddy, you made them yesterday and I even have one in my bag.' Ebuka unzips his small rucksack and pulls out his favourite snack.

'Ah ok. Yes, my son. Yeees… yees… yes. There are plenty of eggs… egged… eggy fishes at the seaside, and we also have some in the cooler.' Chika and Ike chorused, heaving a deep sigh of relief. That is how the name was birthed.

So, Ike made it a routine to prepare these snacks every weekend. He'd make five or six sets that'd last for the whole week.

The process of making egged fish is quite a stressful one for anyone setting out to do it for the first time. Chika initially wasn't interested in learning it, but when circumstances changed, she knew that if she wanted Ebuka to remain happy, she had to do it.

Egged fish is made from freshly mashed boiled potatoes, butter or cheese, milk, salt, pepper, and fish. Firstly, the potatoes are peeled, then boiled. While they boil, a mixture of a small amount of water, milk, butter, or cheese is made. Then a pinch of salt and pepper are added to the mixture.

On the other hand, some fresh eggs are broken, and their contents are emptied into a small bowl and turned. When there are many eggs available, Ike would add them directly into the stock. Else the eggs served for decorating the external part of the snack before baking.

Next, the freshly boiled potatoes are mashed, and a handful of flour is added to make the potatoes more consistent. Afterwards, the stock is added little by little, kneading at each addition until a thick, semi-solid paste is formed. It'll then be the turn of Ike's magic fingers as he shapes the dough into ovoid or egg-shaped structures.

Next, he bores a small hole at the top through which he inserts some pieces of cooked fish. And finally, he rubs some liquid eggs on the external part of the snack and positions them on the frying tray that goes inside the oven. Once they are done baking, they're made to cool and later stored away in a cool place.

***

While Chika warmed the snacks in the microwave, the 6 am alarm rang, and she went to wake Ebuka up.

'Nnam, it's time to wake up to pray and get ready for school,' she says, while gradually peeling the layers of blanket that covers him.

Ebuka stretches himself, slowly opening his eyes. 'Mommy, good morning.'

'Good morning my handsome son. How are you doing and how was your sleep?' Chika responds.

'Mommy, I'm fine. Can I sleep a little more?' he asks

'Nna, no. You'll sleep after school, my dear,' she responds

'But Mom, it's only 6 am and school opens at 8 am. Please just 30 minutes more.'

'My dear, no. Before we get done praying, have you shower, get dressed, eat, and walk down to school, it'll be 8 already. So, get up and brush your teeth while I package your snacks.' Chika concludes.

Ebuka slowly gets up and walks to the bathroom to brush his teeth while Chika tidies up her documents and other items she'd need for this all-important day, including going through her responses for the interview.

Afterwards, they prayed together, ate, and walked to Ebuka's school, a few blocks away from the house.

'Nnam, Mommy will be late today, so I won't be able to pick you up after school.' Chika tells Ebuka as they walk to school.

'Mommy why?' Ebuka asks.

'Mommy has an important appointment today at the office. They want to promote mommy to a higher position. And mommy has worked so hard for this new position. So, I'll be spending time talking to more people today than other times.' Chika tries to explain.

'But Mommy, you can still finish on time before school dismisses. Or you can come and take me to your office, and I'll wait for you.' Ebuka insisted.

'Yes, Nnam. If I finish before school closes, I'll come to take you to the office. But I have also asked grandpa to come to pick you up in case I don't finish on time.'

'Grandpa is coming?!' Ebuka asks, visibly joyful.

'Yes Nnam, he's coming.' Chika responded.

'No problem then. You can talk to many people and get the new office while I stay with grandpa.' Ebuka added excitedly.

'Guess what Nnam?'

'What Mom?' Ebuka says smiling.

'Grandpa will be staying with us for some weeks. And grandma is also coming over in the next few days.'

'That's great! I've always wanted to see grandma, but I didn't want to tell you because you've been busy. And I didn't want to disturb you.'

'It's alright dear. They'll both be here for some time. And whenever you want to ask anything, just ask, ok?'

'Ok, Mom.'

'That's my son. Alright Nnam, it's time to go see Miss Ifunanya.'

'Yes. I love you, Mom.'

'I love you so much Nnam.'

They kiss themselves and say goodbye as Ebuka enters the school gate. Chika picks her bike and cycles to the office. Her office is just downtown, ten minutes away from home.

***

The Director of National Intelligence (DNI) has just arrived to meet with his deputy before the scheduled meeting with Dr Chika. The deputy director is in the operation's room taking briefings from heads of various departments under the agency.

As the driver pulls up, one of the officers quickly reaches for the back door so the Director could get down.

'Good morning, Sir,' the officer says standing at attention.

'Good morning Onyema, how're you doing today?' he replies.

'Everything is good Sir. You're welcome to the office today,' the officer says as they climb the stairs that lead into the building.

The National Intelligence Agency coordinates the various agencies involved in the antiterrorism operations on behalf of the federal government. The headquarters is a five-story edifice of the 18th-century, designed after the style of the famous Italian architect Andrea Palladio. Located in the heart of the city, the building has grown to become a landmark for the entire city, as tourists often come around to admire its splendour.

Around the house is an ornamental garden designed by the popular Igbo interior designer Cabiojinia. It has two fountains on both the east and west wings of the building. And because of its location, residents would often come around to sit and chat, or just to take a walk in the cool of the day, after stressful hours of work.

This is besides the journalists that always flock around the area, especially after the recent antiterrorism operation, where a major leader of a terror group was captured. This meant there was a potential risk of attack on the agency, and so several security guards were always around the building to ward off any over-curious eyes.

The Director walks down to the central operations room while he asks officer Onyema to leave his briefcase and other items in his office on the 4th floor.

As he enters the room, everyone stands to salute. 'Good morning, Sir,' his deputy says.

'Good morning, Fred, what do we have this morning?' the Director smilingly replies.

Fred goes on to illustrate the various missions on course in various parts of the country and the world.

'At the moment we have twenty-seven operations on course. We'll likely be adding six more today because Mr Fisher is back in the country, so we want to follow him closely after the latest reports we received from the Mi6. We're also about to close two operations this morning.'

'Which operations were you about to close?' The Director asked.

'One is the operation regarding Chief Zikog.' Fred replies.

'And why should we close it?' The Director quizzed.

'We saw that it was a false alarm. Contrary to what we were told by the local agents, Chief Zikog never left his country that evening. It seems that some corrupt officials were paid by his men to send us wrong info so he can escape to Nzupita, a country to the south. We got the info that he is at the border now, so...'

'I told you never to trust those men.' The director cuts in. 'Let's quickly inform our agents. We need to reactivate Operation Spider immediately. We shouldn't let him enter Nzupita because that would mean disappearance for another 6 months to one year. And I can't afford to end my tenure without getting that wicked murderer. I've chased him for almost 4 years, and we can't afford any mistakes.'

'Sure Sir. We'll get him this time.' Fred responds, nodding his head.

'So, how about the six operations you're considering adding to the list?' The Director continues.

While Fred was presenting the new operations, the Director sees Chika sitting in her office across the hallway. Chika is going through some documents regarding the last antiterrorism operation she conducted a couple of weeks ago. She coordinated one of the most successful operations of her career. It was the capture of

Selence, the terror lord of the East. It was an operation that earned her a lot of praise and admiration from colleagues and recommendations from superiors, and she thinks it's time to ride on the wave of that to the position she deserves.

After Fred was done with the briefing, the Director desired to know how the recently concluded operations coordinated by Chika went. As they were about to begin playing the footage of the operation, he asks that Chika be called into the room. The interview process was about to begin, and Chika was fully aware.

Dressed in her classic elegant clothing (a little below knee-length skirt and a well-tailored fit button-down shirt made of silk), Chika smiled at the junior officer that was sent to call her. She's always been the cheerful type since her days of internship at the Defence Institute; a quality that endeared her to most of her colleagues, besides her unmatched work ethic. Whenever there was a special operation that had Chika as the team leader, many officers would love to be part of it. She was charismatic, disciplined and results oriented. If you wanted to learn something, you just had to be in her team.

It was not always like this, especially at the beginning, as some colleagues often tried to demean her role because she was a woman. She soon put them in their place, and since then, it's hard not to admire her, especially her ability to foresee the intricacies of an operation and her depth of time-stamped planning.

Chika had never lost any colleague during an operation since she became a team leader and now as a squad leader. But this last operation was different; a complicated feat that she knew the risks very well but still accepted. 'We always know the risks, but the risks don't know us,' she always repeats to her squad before each operation.

Chika had been charged to lead a group of five highly experienced A-level officers to Zumkin, a country in the East, known not only for her flourishing agricultural terrains and technological advancement but also her reputation as the hideout of terrorists.

***

Zumkin has been a peaceful country since its formation in the 1700s. Located close to the river Tigris, its mountain range is one of the best ski locations on the planet. Known for its export of all sorts of agricultural produce, everyone in the country seems to be rich or at least have enough to stay comfortable. They held no elections but were simply governed by a group of seven chieftains (Nsalas as they're called) from the seven tribes that composed this secluded country; a tradition they had maintained since inception but which some distant powerful countries have always frowned at.

They were secluded from the international community and had laws that they considered fair and just but have been object of debate internationally. One of such laws, which was the major reason for the operation that Chika was to lead, is their refusal to extradite anyone to anywhere. Provided that you don't commit any crime in their land, you're protected.

Anyone that comes into Zumkin is shielded and enjoys the same benefits as the citizens of this beautiful country. You could marry and raise your family in peace. But once you contravene their laws, the penalty is often draconian. It was such a rule that made it a kind of hideout for ex-warlords and leaders of terrorist organisations, who after their reign of terror always sought a way to reach Zumkin, fully assured that their lives and families would be safe, although money laundering is strictly prohibited.

So, according to intelligence, Selence, the spearhead of a deadly terrorist organisation in his home country, had escaped to Zumkin a couple of months ago. Despite numerous attempts to get him extradited, the Nsalas vehemently refused, citing their laws in defence.

Chika was called in to lead Operation Harbinger. She had visited Zumkin a couple of years ago on holiday with her husband, Ike. During what should have been a romantic holiday, they spent some hours of the day spying on their host and trying to create a map of the place in case they were sent on an operation here in the future. Well, the day has finally arrived, and Chika is returning to this beautiful country to do something that wasn't so beautiful – capture or kill Selence.

From Pirro's international airport to Zumkin would normally take about twenty hours on a commercial flight, with two transits. But with a military jet, the squad will be in Zumkin in about three hours, with no transits nor control towers; straight to the target and out of the country in thirty minutes. The location of Selence has been identified, and hopefully, he'll maintain his routine of sleeping in the bunker just underneath his kitchen tonight. That would aid the operation in no small way and reduce casualties on both sides.

The day arrived and Operation Harbinger was underway.

'Hello everyone. You already know me and how I work. And I know that you are with me.' Chika began.

'We have spent a couple of weeks preparing for this, and we all have the info we need. You all need no motivation; that's for those lazy people warming their cold derrière on the armchairs on Pirro's lane.' Chika gesticulated as she spoke with her characteristic smile. The squad chuckled.

'We are not them and don't wish to be. We just need to get into this beautiful country and uproot the bad seed. We hope not to roast the seed, but if so, so be it. So, help us, God.' Chika concluded.

'Hey, Braze, say a word of prayers for us and the bad seed.'

Braze is the prayer conductor of the team. Everyone just loved his characteristic prayer line as it was often the calm before the storm.

'Heavenly Father, thank you for how busy You are, doing good things in heaven. But most importantly, thank you for choosing us to take care of the bad things for You on earth. Keep us alive and please, take the bad seeds with You.' And they all chorused 'Amen.'

Operation Harbinger was underway as the military jet took off. After a few hours, the team landed on one of the maize fields outside the city and moved by foot to the residence of the dreaded lord of the East. Stopping hundreds of metres away from his residence was done intentionally to avoid being noticed by the security outfit of the Zumkins.

After about seven minutes and 33 seconds, they were at the residence of Selence. Everything from the arrival to his capture went as Chika and her team had planned. It was 3 am, so everyone was in bed, and the squad had to use only a few bullets to neutralise the three guards around the house. Other than that, every other thing went well; Selence was sleeping in his bunker as thought. Once captured, he was handcuffed, and his mouth taped.

'Listen, everyone, the Package is secured and ready to fly. Be on the alert. The difficult side begins now. Let's go!' Chika orders her men as they begin the most difficult part of Operation Harbinger.

They quickly leave the house and head towards the border, where a vehicle was waiting to extract them. Navigating across the highly secured border is both complicated and intimidating, especially at night. Chika knew the terrain, having been here some years back, but much had changed since then. Some houses have been constructed, and the road networks are a lot different from the map they had.

Nonetheless, they pushed on until a few metres away from the border when they heard the foot sound of someone approaching from behind. They quickly took formation but couldn't see anyone. They waited until the sound faded.

As they arose to walk briskly across the border, there was a shot, and Braze was injured. The security forces of Zumkin had been alerted by an injured guard, and they decided to search for the intruders.

Chika and her squad quickly assisted Braze while firing some shots in the direction of the bullet that hit him. They kept moving towards the border while the home security forces advanced, shooting. During the exchange, Braze was shot again on his thigh, and he couldn't walk. One of the members helped him as two others dragged Selence across the border. They soon reached the vehicle that was waiting for them just beyond the border and zoomed off with shots being fired by the Zumkin security forces. Unfortunately, Braze died of bleeding en route to the military base.

***

While they watched the footage, the director would intermittently look at Chika while stroking the side of his hair with the back of his fingers. At the end of the footage, he asked Chika to meet him in his office while he finishes up with his deputy.

'Please, do wait for me in my office. I'll be there in a moment,' he signals with his hands.

He discharges his deputy after a couple of minutes, asking about the time of the meeting with the Senate

Committee on Intelligence. They agree to meet some minutes before the meeting to finetune their answers.

Chika rises to leave, more worried than when she entered the room. That operation had indeed earned her the respect of her colleagues, including the top officers at the agency and in politics, but watching the footage again made her think if she hadn't made a lot of mistakes during the operation. The fact that the Director didn't say anything, and his body language didn't help matters.

She slowly walks to her office in sober reflection. She needed some reassurance, she wanted someone to talk to, but not anyone. Someone who understands how operations work but also understands her very well. Someone who she trusts, someone who has the right words, someone like Ike.

But Ike isn't around. Ike is not physically close to her. Ike is just on a frame on her table smiling while her ear aches for his voice, while her heart yearns for his words.

CHAPTER 3

While Chika mused over the meeting with the Director and yearned for some soothing words, she suddenly caught herself as she remembered that she should be at the Director's office.

Chika stood just outside the office of the Director thinking of several unrelated things at the same time. Her mind went from her late husband, Ike to Ebuka, from Dede to her career, from her office desk to her shoes … just random uninterrupted thoughts that spent only a few seconds in focus before giving way to another.

The Director soon arrived after the meeting with his deputy. The door to his office is locked with a double security check; the first is his fingerprint and then a code made of a combination of numbers and letters. He opens the door and with his hand beckons Chika to come in.

His office is a sparsely decorated one with a few pieces of furniture. Made of wooden floors, the office decor is a mixture of ancient and modern. While the roof, walls and other electronic gadgets are state of the art, the windows, doors, and other items of furniture either date back to the '50s or were refurbished with materials that date back to that time.

The main desk is a dark brown piece of furniture made from the ancient Bururu tree that grows majorly in tropical regions. Long three metres and 150 centimetres wide, the oval-shaped table is 15cm thick with smooth golden edges. In front of the table is a carving of a running lion on grass.

On the wall are portraits of the regional Governor and the President hanging beside that of the Director. A few metres away is an antique walnut comodino, with the photograph of his family comfortably sitting on top. By the sides and behind the desk are three windows that are approximately 135cm long each with grey blinds, which he rarely uses by the way. He prefers the white silk curtains that keep the place warm and help spread the light evenly across the room. Then, behind this main table is a wooden armchair.

The exciting thing about this whole setup is that the chair is the cheapest item in the room – just a little above 15 dollars. And the Director will always tell the story of the chair to anyone that crosses that entryway; it's sort of a nice way to start a conversation that sometimes can be quite tense along the way.

**

It's rumoured that one of the days, the Senate President came to visit him because of a bill that was about to pass in Congress. The Senate President was his schoolmate at the prestigious Cabiojinia University in Pirro. They both studied law and along the line became very good friends, although they chose different career paths.

While the Senate President explained the bill and its effects on the socio-political system of the country, he simply listened, nodding at intervals, but without uttering a word. When the Senate President finished, the Director simply began telling him the story of his armchair. Rumour has it that at the end of listening to this long 'interesting' story, the Senate President changed his mind on the bill. So, the chair, or rather the story behind it has hidden powers to change people's decisions.

The chair is a reminder of his humble beginnings. His grandma got it during his years at St. John's secondary school. Then in school, you had to come with your desk from home. Since he hadn't one, his grandmother stopped by a carpenter that lived nearby and asked him to make one for his grandson. That was her gift to him for successfully getting admitted into secondary school.

After his secondary school education, he left the chair at home as he proceeded to the university. But when he was appointed Director of National Intelligence, he asked a good carpenter to make some adjustments to the chair, while maintaining the original piece of wood used. Whenever he sees or sits on it, he wants the chair to constantly remind him of his roots and how far he has come.

***

'Good morning once again, Miss Chika,' he says as he walks to his table positioned close to the window, on the opposite side of the entrance.

'Good morning, Sir,' Chika responded, standing beside the table in the well-decorated office.

'Alright. Please have a seat.' He says, pointing to the padded ergonomic chair in front of his wide desk.

'Thank you, Sir.' Chika responded.

While he spoke, Chika was still thinking through the entire Operation Harbinger and the possible questions he was going to ask her. 'Ike would have been a perfect tutor. If he were here, we would have rehearsed all the possible questions and figured out the best ways to answer them. But he's not here even to cheer me up. Even to say a word of encouragement,' Chika mused.

Her thoughts were soon interrupted by the words of the Director, 'Would you mind a cup of coffee? I could make for both. As you know, I have a coffee machine right there at the corner. That's one of the advantages that come with the office.' He smiled as he pointed in the direction of a dark Espresso machine, 45° West behind him.

'No Sir, thanks. I had one already this morning, Sir.' Chika politely responded.

The Director adjusts his chair and goes through some files on his desk.

'Miss Chika, what do you think of this?' he gestured at Chika, handing her a piece of paper containing some figures. Chika gently takes the paper and goes through the figures, acting as though she fully understood what it's all about.

'But the figures don't seem to add up.' She spoke.

'Exactly. That's the same thing I told him. I've said several times that this bill can't pass. You can't cut the military expenditure now and in this manner.' The Director cuts in.

Chika nods in agreement and continues to peruse the figures. She was aware that the senate was trying to cut the military expenditure and the amount the various agencies get. But she didn't have the details of where nor how far the cut was going to be.

'Anyway, things will sort themselves out today as we go to see the Senate committee on intelligence,' the Director says as he closes the file and moves it to a corner.

'So, tell me, how have you been and how's your son, Ebuka? He must be a big boy now,' he asks as he walks to the comodino to take a folder.

'I'm doing great Sir. And Ebuka is doing the same. Thanks, Sir.'

'Good to know. What do you think of Operation Harbinger?'

'What?!' For a moment Chika was jolted. She has been relaxed for these few minutes and wasn't expecting that question at all. Her rehearsed lines completely evaporated as she struggled for a moment to articulate a reasonable response.

'I think it was an interesting operation that required some great deal of skill and experience. We tried to do the best we could but unfortunately, I didn't anticipate the shot that was fired at Braze as we attempted to cross the border. I'm deeply sorry about that, Sir.'

'It's ok. It was a difficult Operation. I knew the risks involved and decided to assign the operation to you. I knew you were the best person to coordinate that expedition and you didn't disappoint. I'm deeply sorry for the loss of Braze, but it was impossible to predict that shot.' The Director concluded.

'Alright. I called you because we're creating a special unit that will be detached from here. It'll still be under the supervision of this agency, although you'll be reporting both to me and to someone else that is not directly linked to this agency. It'll be a special antiterrorism unit with a budget and functions that will be highly classified.

When we deliberated the whole thing with the President, most of us on the table had no doubt as to who should coordinate the unit. So, when I proposed your name, they simply agreed; it was as if they were waiting for me to speak so they could chorus. So, Miss Chika here is your immediate appointment from the Presidency. You'll be coordinating the unit with effect from now.

I've scheduled an appointment to meet with the architect designing the new building that will house your office and those of your assistants. He'll be here tomorrow at 10 am so you can see the plan and make your input. We need to erect that structure in less than six months because of the urgency needed. In that building, we'll also have special rooms that will be Code RED. We've decided to separate some confidential issues because of the breach we experienced here last month.' The Director said.

The last words had not left the mouth of the Director before Chika shouted, 'Thank you, Sir! Thank you, Sir. I sincerely appreciate this opportunity to serve, and I'll never disappoint you and the country.' She has contained her excitement all the while. She couldn't hide her joy any longer.

'Chika, as you get into this new office, I want you to always remember where you're coming from and why you are here. You've worked so hard to be where you are today, but never forgetting where you started. Remain focused, treat others fairly and justly, and most importantly, don't allow these politicians down the street to steer you the wrong way. Ours is to serve the nation, theirs is to serve the donors, don't forget that.' He concluded.

***

As she went back to her office, Chika was visibly excited, but she was also a bit sad. She thought of what it would have been to have Ike around to enjoy this rare moment with her. They had both dreamed of excelling in their careers when they first set out. They couldn't have imagined that she would become a director of a unit one day. And a director of a unit that reports directly to the President. That was just too much for her.

Immediately she entered her office, she shut the door behind her and burst into tears. 'Ike, this appointment is for us. We did this together. You sacrificed so much for me to be where I am today. This can only be the reward of the profuse efforts you made while you were here with me,' she muttered as she cried the more.

When she eventually got herself, she called her dad and mom to break the news to them.

'Dad, we made it! Your girl has made it!' she repeats excitedly.

'Yes, my love. I knew you'd make it; that you'd get to where you are now. But be careful, the difficult job begins now. But I'm sure you'll triumph too,' he adds.

'Alright. See you later this evening or over the weekend. I had told Ebuka that you'll be coming to pick him up if I am late at the office, but since I have some time, I'll go pick him up myself. So, you guys can come later this evening or during the weekend.' She spoke.

'Alright, Nnem. I'm so proud of you. God bless and keep you in this new office. You'll shine beyond your imagination. I believe that God will use you to make our country safer and less corrupt.' the mom adds.

'Amen. But Mom, I'm not in the anti-corruption agency. I'm just focused on keeping the country safe.' Chika said.

'Yes, I know. But as a Christian, I know that you won't see corruption in your agency or those in other places and keep calm. You have an obligation to speak out against such practices. So, my daughter, God will use you to eradicate corruption in our system.' Her mother reiterated.

'Ok, Mom. Amen. I'll see you later tonight or during the weekend.'

As Chika dropped the call with her parents, she got a call from the Director's office asking for her presence immediately. She quickly closes the files she was examining and walks to the office of the Director. She was a bit apprehensive because she wasn't expecting to go back to meet with him, seeing that they just finished discussing barely 45 minutes ago.

Standing next to the Director in his office is a dark chocolate young man of medium size and average height. Initially, Chika couldn't classify him, but with the aid of a prototype laying on the Director's table, and the fact that the Director had previously spoken of an appointment with an architect, Chika soon guessed that the young man could be the architect after all.

'Sorry Miss Chika, I had to call you back because the architect came around, and I thought we could meet him at the same time instead of having a different appointment for tomorrow. I'll be leaving for the senate committee hearing soon. So, you two can continue with the various amendments you want to make. Later, you'll relate to me any changes you agreed to.' The Director said.

'It's alright Sir,' Chika responds before turning to greet the architect, Chukwuma. He in turn greets her, and they both move to the general meeting hall to discuss the project in detail, while the Director gets ready for his hearing.

***

In the meeting room, Chukwuma carefully illustrates the project, and for over an hour, Chika spent time asking questions on any detail she deemed fit. And Chukwuma was willing to clarify. When the meeting lasted for over an hour, she thought that it'll be great to take a coffee break and continue later. Chukwuma instead suggested that the meeting be adjourned until tomorrow seeing that he had an appointment on the other side of the town in a few hours. Chika obliged and they agreed to meet at 10 am the next day and maybe go to see the site of the project.

As Chukwuma left the National Intelligence headquarters, Chika quickly ran to her office to get her car keys. For a moment she had forgotten that her son will be expecting her at the school and that grandpa won't be going to pick him up.

She grabs her key and bag and dashes out of the office, cycling down Pirro's lane to Ebuka's school. While cycling to Ebuka's school and reflecting on how her day is unfolding, it dawns on her that this may be the last time she'll be cycling freely without a security detail. As the director of a new unit, she'll be eligible (without choice) to always have two guards with her whenever she's on duty.

***

Ike's death has been shrouded in mystery, at least in Chika's view. She lost her dear husband a couple of years ago and she still can't get over him. The image of their last meeting continues to play in her mind.

It was a normal Thursday evening. Not really... It was a special Thursday evening at the National Intelligence headquarters on Pirro's lane. That didn't come out right either... It was an awesome day for two special people that work together at the National Intelligence headquarters. Yes... that's the best way to put it.

For the entire day, these two lovebirds have texted themselves while remaining undistracted from their high-profile jobs. Their jobs are sensitive if you seriously think about it. On them depends the Intelligence, and so, the security of the entire national infrastructure. So, to think that they'll be exchanging texts like the one below is absurd... or is it not?

Anyway, it was the anniversary, not of their wedding but the meeting anniversary of Chika and Ike. This beautiful family, that is blessed with a son called Ebuka, celebrates every moment. From birthdays to the first days of the month, from the day of giving their life to Jesus Christ to their wedding anniversary. But as written above, they also celebrate the first day they met several years ago under a tree.

At home, they made it an unwritten rule to celebrate every win, no matter how tiny that may seem. No win, no progress, no promotion, no medal was seen as insignificant. Life itself is a great gift from God, why not live each day celebrating life and reminding yourself that the gift won't be here eternally.

Saturday will be their wedding anniversary, so they decided to begin the celebration today. After all, although the day of their wedding fell on a Saturday, the date was today. Ike, as usual, never misses a moment to remind Chika how internally and externally gorgeous she is. It's become a lifestyle for him to make sure that Chika is always happy no matter how bad his day may be going.

In his words, 'when your woman is happy, even the spirit of sadness cannot penetrate. There is nothing as powerful as a happy woman… standing in front of the man.' To think that this quote is inscribed on a 50cm-by-50cm frame hanging behind Ike's desk is hilarious. But to know that the same inscription is his ring tone for every call he receives is just… more than hilarious. But hey, that's Ike's philosophy and as the Holy Scriptures say (paraphrasing), 'Ike has chosen this way, and none can take it from him.'

'Hi Miss Chi, it's me, Master D. How are you doing? Still working?' Ike texts Chika

'Hi Master D. It's me, Miss C. I'm doing great. How about you? I'm just putting some finishing touches on my shoelace while waiting for you.'

'This dinner will be special.' He continues

'Yep. I've been getting ready since Monday. It's been a while, my love.'

'Hmmm… Myself, I've been getting ready for two weeks now ;)'

'That's not true. You don't even have any special clothes for tonight. I'm sure you'll still be on that pink t-shirt… lol' Chika teases him.

'Hahaha… Don't be too sure Darling. You know I can always pull surprises on you when I want to.'

'Oh yes, and I'll be excited to see the surprises you've packaged for tonight and in the coming days.'

'Fair enough. But I'll still be wearing the pink shirt tonight. Just for tonight…lol' Ike adds.

'Hahaha, I knew it, Babe. I knew you were still going to wear that particular shirt. Anyway, I'm not tired of seeing my Sweetheart in them. *Winks.'

'Hmmm… I plan on wearing the same pair of pink trousers.'

'Complete pink? Nna, you'll never change. You've worn this same outfit for five consecutive years… five consecutive meeting anniversaries. Who does that? hahaha.'

'Well, I'll never forget the day I met you under that shade on a warm afternoon. Just like I'll never forget the day you agreed to spend the rest of your life with this stubborn boy. That's why I always love to wear that outfit on special days like this.'

'I know Nnam. I'll never forget the day I saw this crazy but innocent boy under the tree pretending to revise for exams… lol,' Chika adds, blushing.

'And you pretended to be resting on the bench too… hahaha'

'Well, I was there before you, remember?' Chika winks

'Yeah, but you stopped resting the moment you saw me. :)'

'Hahahaha... Fair enough.'

'I will forever love you, Nkem.'

'I will forever love you more Nnem.'

'But there's a new item of clothing though ;)' Ike chips in.

'And what is that? A black belt or a green muffler? lol...'

'Hmmm... a black pair of shoes.'

'A black pair of shoes? Finally, the man I loved that year has decided to add some spice to his delicious meal. *winks'

'So, Nnem, guess which?' Ike asks.

'Hmmm... I can't tell. You know I'm not good at guesses. A moment Darling, I need to submit a file to the Director. I'll be back shortly.' Chika writes.

'Ok Darling. But must you go now? How about your secretary?'

'Nkem, it seems you've forgotten that we're at work... haha. And when did I get a personal secretary? It is people like you that have secretaries naah. Job seekers under probation like us don't... lol' Chika teases him.

'Hahaha... well, I can ask for an exchange. My secretary becomes your secretary, while yours becomes mine.' Ike winks

'No way! You think I don't know that she's been looking at you somehow for some time now. Nope, you'll stay with your male secretary, and I'll stay with mine... lol.' Chika writes.

'Okay. Please go meet the Director; I don't want any queries. *winks' Ike responds.

'Ok. I love you.'

'I love you more.' Ike concludes.

Chika dashes out to submit some reports to the Director. They're intelligence reports she gathered on the recent cyberattacks suspected to come from Zumkin. The attacker hacked into the systems of some government agencies and leaked several classified information to the press.

The Director was just concluding a meeting when Chika arrived. He quickly concludes and asks Chika in. They both discussed the findings and agreed on the necessary steps to take to curtail the damage. A spokesperson for the National Intelligence will address the press that evening while some of the agents involved in a covert operation in Zumkin will be reassigned as their identities have been leaked.

At the end of the meeting, Chika returns to her office to tidy up with some of these assignments seeing she won't be at the office for some days.

'Hey D, I'm back and done with the assignments. Now tell me the black shoes... Oh, wait! Please tell me the black shoes are the ones I got you last month.' Chika writes Ike.

'Hmmm… Yes, my sweet Darling, those exact ones.' Ike replies.

'Wow! I thought you never liked them. I was even planning on returning them when we come back from holidays.' Chika exclaimed.

'Return? I like them. I just didn't want to wear them except for a special occasion. And here is that special occasion. *smiles'

'Now, get your behind to my office so we can go home. Ebuka will be waiting for us while we're here chatting like kids.' Chika replies.

'Well, I don't have issues being a kid… a grown kid anyway… and only with you *winks'

'Yeah, you're my grown man kid… my puppy, my doll.'

'I love you, Sweetheart. *hearts' Ike writes.

'I love you more, my Honeypie *kisses'

Ike had just finished from his office on the third floor and was headed for Chika's office when he got a call from the FBI headquarters that he was urgently needed. Ike had to immediately cancel his scheduled evening engagement with his wife and young child, and together with his driver went to the FBI headquarters.

This isn't the first time Ike has had to cancel his evening routine with his family because of work. Although it can be quite difficult sometimes, Chika always understands. A few times Chika has also had to postpone her return home for office engagements. They both work at the National Intelligence, though in different offices, so, they understood their schedules quite well. They've come to understand that this is how things will go for some years until they get to a point in their career where they determine their schedules to a great percentage.

***

While it has always been Chika's dream to follow the footprint of Dede, her father, in the military, Ike never dreamt of working anywhere close to the Military, Intelligence or Armed forces in general. He was just a young chap that was interested in numbers, data analytics and artificial intelligence. He always dreamed of building the next IBM or at least a corporation that would match its glory, together with his university colleagues. So, together with his friends in school, they began on time to work on their craft.

It was during one of the exhibitions at the university that some members of the National Intelligence noticed him and cunningly offered to sponsor his craft. Ike and his colleagues had developed software that could predict human thoughts and behaviour by simply analysing the last three images the person watched. It was an advancement of the work of Sir Arit Jhuv that studied how an individual's brain encoded recent images, no matter the person's level of consciousness.

Ike and his colleagues had no idea in what field their innovation would find application, but they were however excited to share their knowledge with the visitors at the annual University Expo. Not many people apart from a few company representatives came to the stand where Ike and his friends were playing with their toy. And none of the visitors was that excited to invest in a project that even the developers have no idea of its application. It was only two men who were dressed as though they were off to the beach or some resort, that offered to invest.

Pleasantly surprised by such a show of unfettered interest, Ike and his colleagues agreed to work with them. They wondered whether these investors knew what they were talking about when they offered to invest one hundred million dollars. But curious about the whole thing, and a chance to put their innovation to good use, Ike and his colleagues jumped at the opportunity and completed the paperwork. They'd later realise that they were working for the National Intelligence, and their innovation will be used for things they never imagined.

**

When Ike got the call that he was needed at the FBI headquarters, he quickly sent a message to Chika to ask for permission. The FBI headquarters is located 5km from their office and if everything goes well and quickly, he'd be home in a few hours to join in the celebration.

'I've just been called by the FBI Director. Seems I'll miss dinner with you tonight.'

'Nna, you won't miss it; you'll just be a couple of hours late. It's our anniversary, you know.' Chika pretends to refuse.

'You're right Nnem, I can't miss it. I'm coming down immediately, maybe I should say hi before leaving.'

'Nkem, not maybe. You must kiss me bye before heading to that place.'

'Alright Darling, see you in a minute. *smiles'

'I'm waiting, Ikem.'

Ike quickly gets some files into his briefcase and calls his driver to drive out to the street leading to the main entrance. The call was urgent, and he knew what that meant – there is a problem that needs an urgent solution, and every second counts.

'Hi Darling, let me run along, alright? I'll be with you in a couple of hours' Ike tells Chika as they both kiss goodbye.

No one, not even the best of prophets, could have seen what would happen in the next few hours, and that this might be the last kiss between Ike and his sweet wife Chika.

CHAPTER 4

So, I was there that beautiful Thursday evening when Ike was called to quickly come to the FBI headquarters for an urgent meeting with the Director. I was on Pirro's Lane because I had an important meeting with the Director of National Intelligence.

Ike was exiting the building when I got to the National Intelligence headquarters. He had just kissed Chika goodbye and was headed for his navy-blue BMW car when I bumped into him. We both exchanged greetings and promised to meet when he's back from holiday. Our paths have crossed on a few occasions although we worked in different departments and different buildings too.

As I entered the building, one of the receptionists offered to lead me to the Director's office upstairs. It's been a while since I came here; the last time should be well over 2 years ago.

When we got upstairs, I met an elderly man sitting just outside the office of the Director. I couldn't understand what a man of his age would be doing there at that time. 'Maybe he's a veteran I thought to myself or a pensioner of the National Intelligence who had come to collect his pension.' Don't worry, I know that thought sounds stupid, but that's the least stupid that flew across my mind. I just couldn't understand what a man of his age would be doing here by that time too.

Anyway, I decided to sit next to him while I waited for my turn. 'Who knows how long this would take?' I thought to myself.

Well, the old man seemed not to care really; he was busy reading a book with his legs crossed. It was as if he had a given number of pages to cover before his appointment.

'Good evening, Sir.' I said, attempting to break the ice.

'Good evening, Son. I hope you're vaccinated?' he responded.

I must say that I was surprised by the question. Not like I have anything against vaccines. I mean, I'm fully vaccinated and even had a nose mask on. Anyway, I answered him respectfully, 'Yes, Sir.'

'That's good my son. Now you can come closer, there's something I want to tell you.'

The elderly man adjusted his seat and began looking at me cheerfully. At first, I was a bit surprised because his attitude now is a stark opposite to what he displayed when I arrived. He lowered his nose mask and in a deep fatherly tone began to reel out some gems.

'My son,' he began. 'I see that you're a bright young chap who I suppose wants to travel far in life and career.' I nodded in affirmation.

'So, how far do you want to go?' he quizzed

I told him how I want to become a great military surgeon. I'm currently training at Cabiojinia's Heart Institute in the neighbouring city. I told him how my dream has always been to help our brave men and women in uniform. And that someday I'd love to become the Director of the World Health Organisation.

He smiled as I said all these. And then he continued with his counsel. 'You see, my son, all these are quite achievable. But you must be willing to do what it takes to get there. Not bad things of course. But you must know that every position you aspire for requires a price that you need to pay to get there.' He added

'My son, I'd like to give you some things that have helped me get thus far in life. You may choose to leave them, but I think you should pick a few from the list. I call it *when you want to travel far, travel heavy*. I know that this goes against the popular opinion of *if you want to travel far, you should travel light*. I'll tell you about that in Part 2.

IF YOU WISH TO TRAVEL FAR, TRAVEL HEAVY

Now, here are some things you'll need to either travel with or buy while travelling. Without them, hmmm… the journey of life may be impossible to stay in.

1. God

Develop an intimate relationship with Him early, and never let go of Him no matter what you face. Of all things I'll tell you, son, this is the most important. If you're with Him, you'll always be in the majority. Know

Him, Love Him, Cherish Him. Let Him be The Guide of your life and you won't regret a moment. That's all I can say about that. You'll discover the rest by yourself.

2. Love

Oh, my son, you need lots and lots and lots of this. Stuff a good space of your vehicle with this. Love unconditionally. Do not expect anything in return when you do. Be genuine about it – just love people for who they are. All that a man has he will leave behind, but all that a man did will go with him. At the end of the day, what will count is how many lives you inspired and touched for good.

3. Relationships

Friends are some of the most important items you can ever have in your life. The world is a selfish place, not necessarily because people hate you. But because everyone is busy chasing their destinies. But if you can find people who love you for who you are and your purpose align, and they're willing to die for you, then cherish such relationships and never let them go. Just a few of them is enough. But you need them because you can't grow nor thrive in isolation.

4. Wisdom

My son, the Holy Book says that wisdom is the principal thing to get. So, please, pursue her, chase her, get her, and keep her. She will exalt you and guide you throughout your journey. You may not have it at home, but before you travel far, buy some along the way.

5. Originality

I won't say that you should be yourself because you are born in sin, and as a fallen man, you could have all forms of nastiness. So, don't be yourself. Rather, being original is different. Being original means being exactly what God created you to be. And in that case, I'd say this: understand who you are in God and remain originally that unapologetically. Imitation is for people who are yet to understand themselves. You are unique. You are different. You are special. Just like everyone else.

6. Joy and Happiness

My son, be joyful always. Be happy always. I know it's going to be quite difficult to be because several things would want to make you angry and bitter daily. But you must refuse to give in to them. Therefore, you need to derive your source of joy from the Holy Spirit and your happiness from things outside material things that perish. Find joy in the little things people often ignore and be genuinely happy.

7. Gratitude

This is important to have my child. Travel heavy with gratitude. Be grateful to God for everything. Be grateful to your parents for the little they provide. Be grateful to friends, colleagues, neighbours etc. Show gratitude to anyone that helps you. Don't only think about it, show it. Gratitude keeps the doors of blessings open for more.

8. Faith

Carry a good dose of faith, my son. This journey seems short but it's far. You'll need him a lot throughout your journey. Remember, I said faith.

9. Courage

Oh, my son, I almost forgot. Please take courage along with you. Its importance cannot be overemphasised. To get to your destination, you'll need loads of it. You'll certainly meet with several obstacles along the way, but courage will ask you to keep going forward. And the more you overcome, the more you're strengthened for the other challenges ahead.

10. Trust

Inasmuch as you don't trust everyone, you must carry Trust along with you on this journey. Wisdom will help you to differentiate who to trust from who not to trust. But know that you must have people you trust; without trust, you won't have stability in your relationships.

11. Moderation

Please my son, importantly, take moderation with you. You need it before and after you've become great. Before you become great, so you are not spending excessively. And after you become great, so you aren't hoarding unnecessarily. Be moderate in your speech, looks and your temperament.

12. Discipline and consistency

You won't get to your expected end if you aren't consistent and disciplined. Those two elements are important if you must arrive at your destination. As you have set out a target for yourself, don't look sideways, don't be distracted by the noise on the streets. There are many noisemakers on the way who are not going anywhere at all. Leave the noise and focus on your journey.

13. Family

Ehee... Please my dear son, in all you do, always make family your priority. All your achievements will mean nothing if your family is in disarray. All your accomplishments will be wasted if your spouse and child(ren) don't partake in them. Biko, carry them with you – they'll support you, correct, edit your ideas, and above all, love you. Always come home even when you're sad and angry. Once the home front is secured, you'll be better focused on your journey.

14. Patience

Consider all your efforts as seeds that need time to germinate; need watering to grow; need nurturing to mature and yield fruits. So, between the seed time and the harvest, you'll need lots of patience because the tendency is to become frustrated when it isn't sprouting or to rush the fruits when they aren't mature yet. So, please, don't leave patience at home. If you don't have one in your store, please buy one on the way. Lots of it.

15. Forgiveness

You'll certainly make some mistakes along the way because you're human. Therefore, leaning on God and possessing wisdom is extremely important. However, when you make mistakes, learn to admit them, and correct them if possible. But most importantly, learn to forgive yourself afterwards. Don't be paralysed by your mistakes, rather learn from them. Also, learn to forgive others quickly. Anger can become a big clog on your wheel of progress if you let it.

16. Humility

This is one thing that you can't do without. If you don't have it, please buy it immediately you start. Just like wisdom, humility will exalt you beyond your imagination.

17. Respect

Every creature of God should be treated with respect irrespective of race, gender, social, academic, spiritual, or political status. Every child and adult, poor and rich, educated and non, white, and black, male, and female deserve respect.

18. Fast, Pray and Praise

Fasting is both a religious exercise and good for your health when done in the right measure. Some issues require that you fast and pray. Even Jesus Himself said it. Then there are matters that you simply need to praise God for, confessing in faith that they are solved. However, not everything requires prayers. Wisdom will help you know them.

19. Justice

Don't be silent in the face of oppression. Don't turn a deaf ear to the cries of the poor nor blind eyes to the oppression of the weak. The salvation of some people is in your hands. When you see violence, silence is never an option. And never give up on your values and on doing what is right. People may hate, but that is not your business. Stand for justice and be at peace with yourself when you do what is right before God.

20. Money

I know you were waiting for me to say this too. Well, I purposely left it out for the last because it's important but not the most important. Now, God is the most important. But please, get money. Don't believe people who tell you that you don't need it. You do. But be careful, if you love it, then you'll be taking the wrong route. Work very hard or as young people would say, work smart. Get the money that is sufficient for yourself, your family and those in need in your environment. Some things become easier to do when you have money. But remember, money isn't the goal, it's a currency just like many others.

Alright, son, I wish I could continue in this interesting conversation with you, but I need to hurry along. I have a flight to catch. Hopefully, we can continue our conversation when we next meet. Or you can contact me via mail if you have further questions.

Thanks for your attention, my son. God be with you as you journey through life.

All the while he talked, I was just focused on the things that came out of his wise lips. I couldn't believe my eyes. How did God know that I needed to hear these words today? I came to the office to meet the Director for my letter of appointment as an assistant medical director to one of our hospitals once I'm done with my residency. I had known a few of these items the old man talked about. In fact, I have some of them in my trunk. But hearing them afresh was so refreshing.

Thank you, old man. And see you soon, hopefully.

CHAPTER 5

The FBI headquarters is the most prominent building on Quib's avenue. Named after one of the founding fathers of the city, Quib's avenue was one of the quietest places to live in. But that was before the federal government decided that the peace the residents enjoyed was too much and decided to add a little bit of Chaos to the environment.

Although the government always argues that the original city plans included having several high rising buildings in the area, the residents have always challenged such a view with documents that prove otherwise. The case had ended in court a few times but was finally resolved with good compensation to the residents. Many of the people relocated and sold their lands and houses over to the government, who then erected some skyscrapers, including the FBI headquarters there.

Standing tall above other buildings, the FBI headquarters is a structure that many architects, designers and students come to study for its beauty, design, and concept. Constructed with the best materials, the building is completely anti-seismic.

ROOM 39

It was designed by Gima Nakuto, originally from Sink, but naturalised in the country. She had gotten the idea of the building by observing the Mediterranean mussel. That sounds weird but that's what she said in an interview a few years ago about the inspiration for the building.

She's always loved the Mediterranean diet, which by the way is one of the healthiest out there. So, on one of her travels to Sicily, she stayed in a very nice hotel. Unfortunately, that evening the restaurant served her a meal that tasted very bad, so she decided to go eat outside instead. It was late, but about 200m away, there was this small but cosy restaurant. It wasn't as big as the hotel's restaurant where she had lodged, it had about 50 eating spots, but it was well organised.

Everything looked natural and ancient but clean, polished, and very comfortable, not to talk about the dewy perfume and the jazz music that combed the hairs on your ears literally. It was just... how do you say it? Yes, heavenly, immortal.

When she sat down to eat, she didn't need the menu. All she just wanted was whatever was cooking in the kitchen. I mean, you can't have a place like this that smells aphrodisiac and not have meals that match; that would be beyond weird. The waiter didn't need orders, she knew exactly what Mademoiselle wanted and went for it – a plate of Spaghetti allo scoglio and fresh non-alcoholic wine, home-brewed by Chibyke himself.

Sorry, I forgot to tell you that the restaurant is very popular around the major Islands of Italy – Ristorante Celeste di Chibyke. It was during that heavenly supper, that Gima had the inspiration to construct a building that is shaped like the shell of a mussel. When she was eventually contacted to design the FBI headquarters, she knew exactly what she wanted to display on the ground and sky of Quib's Avenue.

***

Ike has just arrived at the FBI headquarters to meet with the Director on this urgent call. On his way, he still found time to send a few tantalising messages to his lovely wife. After the celebration tonight, they'll be travelling to Sicily for a brief weekend vacation. They had booked the trip three months ago and nothing, not even an emergency at work will derail their plans.

The FBI has been trying for several months to use one of the technologies developed by Ike's team to track any person, including innocent citizens. This new technology would bypass any congressional approval. It'll directly infect any device that is connected to the internet.

Several times in the past when this discussion has been held, Ike has always opposed the idea, saying that it limits the privacy of innocent citizens who want to live their normal lives without being spied on by any agency.

Spying anyone should be limited to the antiterrorism act passed by congress that allowed tracking any individual that is considered a potential terrorist. Outside of this provision, Ike vehemently opposes tracking anyone.

The FBI on the other hand wanted to monitor some illegal activities that have been going on around the city for some time now. The perpetrators didn't quite fit the description of terrorists because they were involved in the synthesis and sale of hard drugs, as well as prostitution. So, the FBI wanted to use this to track them. Ike's view is that other instruments could be used to arrest them, which instruments the FBI considers insufficient.

However, some corrupt FBI agents, captained by Mbe, were against this idea of tracking, not for good reasons like Ike, but because they didn't want their evil doings exposed. So, when they learnt that Ike was summoned to the headquarters to activate the programme, they quickly plotted to kill him before he'll be able to do so.

On reaching the FBI headquarters, Ike was invited to the meeting room, where the FBI Director and the Director of National Intelligence were seated, with their assistants.

'Ike, we invited you because we think it's wise to let you in on our main reason for wanting to activate the program. Yes, we wish to track the Collingahs (a name used for the men from Collingah involved in illegal businesses), but the main issue is the internal problem we have,' he said.

'For some months now,' he continued, 'we have observed that some FBI officers are involved in illegal practices in connivance with the Collingahs. We've monitored them and identified a few of them, but we want to get to the leader of that group. We can't continue this way.'

Ike was initially reluctant to comment on this new development. But when he viewed the tapes that have been recorded over the months, he was convinced that the rot was very deep and needed to be eliminated from the root. Even some officers at the National Intelligence agency were involved. It runs deeper than was early thought.

So, Ike agreed that there was a need to internally deploy the program for a limited time and for a limited group of people. There should be no widespread, indiscriminate usage. And once the chain of command was unravelled, the program would be terminated. Once these limits were defined, Ike agreed that the program should be deployed. He agreed to return to the office immediately and get the program activated the same night before leaving for his house.

***

Based on this agreement, Ike leaves the meeting room and calls his driver to come to the entrance. As they headed back to the office, a black car parked outside the building began to follow them. Ike observed this but didn't want the driver to panic. So, he asked him to simply drive faster so he could meet his appointment with his wife.

Close to the office is a bridge of 700m long that links both sides of the town; it's not quite deep, so it's normal to find fishermen late in the evenings coming around to thrust their nets for a catch. As they drive across the bridge, a police vehicle stops them for a search and asks the driver and Ike to come down.

The driver opens the door without questions and gets down. Then advances to the back door to open the door where Ike was sitting. Ike was surprised at the speed with which his driver complied. Normally, the driver would have shown his Identity card and would have explained that he was carrying an officer of the National Intelligence. Also, why would he be so quick to come behind to open Ike's door? Anyway, Ike complied and got out of the car.

He then tries to explain to the police officer that he is a member of the National Intelligence agency and that if he needed any documents, he was willing to provide them. That he is on a national assignment and needs to get to his office immediately.

As he tried to explain, his supposed driver advanced backwards and with speed pulled out a syringe with which to inject him. Ike quickly reads that move and turns around quickly. As they began to struggle, he discovered that the person wasn't his driver but a person he had never met. He could hear someone shout from the police vehicle, 'don't shoot him.'

Some of the corrupt FBI agents had tracked him from the headquarters and disguised themselves as police officers. His driver had been injected with a soporific drug while Ike was meeting with the Director of the FBI and DNI. That's the same drug this corrupt officer wants to inject Ike with. The plan is to put them to sleep and then cause their car to go off the rail. That way, it'd seem like an accident caused by sleep.

When the attempt to inject Ike wasn't working, one of the officers brought out a knife to stab Ike's hand. Mistakenly, he cut Ike's face. As he bled, they quickly had him injected and put him inside the car, set the car on fire and caused it to run off the rail into the river. The corrupt officers quickly removed any evidence from the scene and drove away.

When the rescue team arrived, they only found Ike's driver lifeless. He had been put inside the boot of the car. So, when the car fell into the river, he was still in a temporary coma and couldn't get out and drowned in the process. Ike's body wasn't found even after an intensive three-day search.

The police investigation uncovered that the driver had issues with insomnia and had taken pills that night before the incident. So, it was concluded that he may have slept off while driving across the bridge and died. The FBI opened an investigation into the incident, but no new evidence has emerged since then. And years have rolled by.

ROOM 39

PART TWO

Some things don't change

ROOM 39

CHAPTER 6

Chika has now assumed office as a director, although she still stayed in her present office at the National Intelligence, pending the completion of the new site.

Recently, as part of the job, she chanced on a file that detailed the illicit activities of the Collingahs and how they were conniving with some corrupt FBI agents to carry out their illegal business. It wasn't directly linked to her office, so she wasn't willing to dig further.

But somehow, she got interested in the tracking system that was to be employed in the investigation. Chika was interested in understanding this program seeing that her unit would make use of it in its operations. After going through the file, she asked one of her unit members to study the files deeper and get back to her soonest.

A few days later, what she learned would shock her. And would define how the coming months of her career would go. When the officer she had assigned the file to reported back to her, she discovered that the program was similar to what Ike had spoken to her about some years ago. She got curious and began to dig deeper into it by herself. She soon found out that some members of the FBI weren't happy about the activation of the program. Her curiosity led her to hypothesise that Ike could have been killed because of something similar. She couldn't lay hands on anything as everything seemed cloudy in her mind.

So, she decided to begin piecing the pieces together. She went from the program Ike developed several years ago to the night of his death. The text messages they had exchanged while he headed to the FBI headquarters, to the scene of his presumed death. She sought to obtain the forensic report of the death of Ike's driver. Some things made sense, but several things weren't adding up. Chika decided to run a parallel investigation at home to unravel what truly happened that night.

***

One evening as Chika was having dinner, a knock was heard at the door. It was 8pm and Chika wasn't expecting any visitors that night. She wondered who it could be that came around. She didn't want to open the door but on second thought she decided to. 'Maybe Dede decided to bring Ebuka back,' she thought. But that was improbable seeing that Ebuka went to stay with him on holiday just yesterday. It's a long vacation and the entire family had travelled to the mountainous countryside for a few weeks of relaxation. Chika went to drop Ebuka off yesterday and return because of her work. So, there was no way Dede would be coming to visit tonight. Also, they could have called her if they were coming.

Chika slowly walked to the door and inquired who it was. A man responded and said that he was Mbe. He said that he had dropped a friend off and decided to stop by to greet the family. Chika knows Mbe, he used to be friends with Ike before things turned sour and Ike decided to sever the friendship.

'Can I come in?'

'Sure, you can.' Chika smiles as she slowly walks back into the house, leaving the door open for Mbe to come in.

Mbe forces a smile in return as he brushes off his shoes before getting in. 'The house is quite warm. Such a great refuge during this cold winter.'

'Just like almost all the houses in the country, you mean?' Chika responds

'Yeah. But nothing beats the house of my director. It's so warm and cosy.' Mbe retorts as he hangs his thick black leather winter jacket on a wooden rack adjacent to the door.

'So, would you mind a cup of hot water on this very cold winter evening as well?' Chika asks sarcastically as she advances to the kitchen.

'Yes, a hot tea if you wouldn't mind.' Mbe responds, as his eyes wander through the photos and other objects on the wall and around the rooms leading to the kitchen.

As Chika readies the tea, she slowly tucks in a sharp kitchen knife in her gown. Since she began her private investigation into the circumstances surrounding the death of her husband, she has had to be more careful with everyone except some trusted friends and assistants. She was determined to get to the root of the matter. At first, she didn't want to admit Mbe into the house, but she thought it'd be an opportunity to ask Mbe some questions seeing that he works with the FBI and maybe was there the night Ike came for a meeting at the FBI headquarters.

'Your tea is ready. I'm also adding a few slices of bread though you didn't ask for it. I also have butter. And my entire collection of beverages is on the table. You can serve yourself as always. Let me get something upstairs that I'm sure you'll like.' Chika said.

Mbe nods in agreement as he walks aimlessly around the kitchen and to the dining table. Chika runs upstairs to shut the door to the room where she has been keeping the pieces of information she gathers on her private investigation, being careful not to have been followed by Mbe. It's a small room with an entrance from the master bedroom. Originally intended to be a prayer room for Ike and his wife, Chika has now transformed it into her secret room. No one, not even Ebuka goes in there.

As Chika went upstairs, Mbe walked around the rooms and finally came and stopped at the stairs, as if waiting for Chika. When Chika opens the door to come down, she was surprised to see him standing there and asks why he wasn't seated eating. Mbe tells her that he wanted to admire her beauty as she ran down the stairs. Chika couldn't understand what he was talking about.

'Please, get back to the table. The tea is getting cold. Remember it's a cold winter evening and you need something quite warm that only a director's house can give.' Chika says as she points Mbe back to the kitchen.

As they sat down to eat, Mbe seemed to be more interested in complimenting the looks of Chika and saying all sorts of sweet things to her. Chika on the other hand was waiting for the right moment to bring up the discussion on Ike's death. When she saw that Mbe wasn't going to stop saying nonsense to her ears, she cut in, this time more decisively.

'Mbe, you're yet to tell me what happened to your lovely friend. Several years have passed and you seem not to be ready to talk about the death of someone you call your best friend.'

'Oh, come on Chika. You know that Ike was my best friend. I mean, I was there when you guys were wedded and when you had your child Ebuka. Of course, he was, and you know it. I just don't want to talk about his death because it hurts me so much, just the same way it hurts you. I just want to move on. I think that's best for you. And I'm here to be a shoulder you can lean on.'

'Fine. But you've never even spent a minute since the incident to tell me what you know about the meeting at the FBI office. Each time I've asked you, you'd often shrug it off as if it was a regular briefing that took place that day.' Chika insisted

'But that's because I don't know. It's highly classified information.' Mbe replied.

'You can't tell me that. With your level at the FBI, you have access to certain classified information. We both know that.' Chika insisted further.

'Exactly. Certain classified information. Not every classified information. What happened that night is a top-secret that only a few people are supposed to know.' Mbe noted.

'And who are the few people?' Chika asked.

'The FBI director and the Director of National Intelligence, I suppose. But what does it matter? You can never get to know these things.' Mbe said.

'How do you mean that I can never get to know? What are you hiding from me Mbe? Speak! Speak Mbe. What are you hiding from me?' Chika raised her voice.

'I'm not hiding anything. But let me warn you, the more you go deep into these things, the more you'll get yourself hurt. And you may end up like Ike!' Mbe said, with a stern voice.

'What did you just say? So, you know certain things regarding the death of someone you call your friend, yet you hide them from me?' Chika asks angrily.

'Calm down Chika. Calm down!' Mbe shouts at her before recollecting himself. 'You see Darling, you need to forget about Ike. He's dead, he's gone. Unfortunately, but that's the truth. You need to move on with your life. And that's why I'm here. I'm here to take good care of you. I was his best friend. I know your needs are emotional and matrimonial. I can make up for them. I can…'

'Oh, shut up!' Chika shouts at him.

'I know you're angry now. Just calm down.' Mbe says as he advances towards her. He tries to hold her hands and move his palms around her shoulders.

'Oh, get your filthy hands off me!' Chika shouts.

'But calm down. We can work things out. Things can work between us. Remember I had my eyes on you even before Ike. I've always admired you from a distance, my love. Ike just came in…'

'Get out of my house! Mbe, I said get out of this house right now! Such a snake of a man. Leave my house immediately and never come back here again. And don't ever send me flowers nor go to Ebuka's school again. I've been calm with you all the while, but that's over.' Chika rebukes him.

'Oh, come on! It hasn't gotten to this point Babe.' Mbe tries to douse the flames.

'Baa what? I said, leave this place immediately! And let me tell you this: whether you like it or not, I'll eventually find out what you are hiding. And when I get to know them, it won't be funny.'

'Alright. As you desire Ma. But I have warned you.'

'For the last time, Leave!' Chika repeats and goes towards the door.

Mbe picks his winter coat and exits the house, as Chika shuts her door loudly. She then goes to her room to weep, while recalling the happy moments she enjoyed with her husband – their first meeting, date, proposal, wedding, vacation, and plans.

A few days later while Chika was at her office with her secretary discussing her schedules, Mbe came around to see her. Initially, she refused to grant him an audience, but after much insistence, she obliged and allowed him in. Mbe comes in and pleads for forgiveness for what transpired the other night. Chika told him that she had forgiven her but warned him never to come close to her house again. If he had anything regarding the death of Ike that he wants to discuss, he can come to the office. Else, he should keep a distance from her.

***

The construction of the Quartier Générale of the antiterrorism unit is now three months in its construction. Most of the offices are ready including the ones that will serve as Code RED. Beating the initial estimate of six months, Chukwuma was ready to deliver the project in four.

This is the biggest project Chukwuma has ever handled. Although he is specialised in the design and construction of highly security-oriented buildings, the other projects he has handled in the past were nothing close to this, maybe except for the 5.6 billion dollars mansion of the Saudi Royal family. The rest were just projects below that amount but not less complex in their function nor less important in their use.

Some of them are the Headquarters of Mossad of Israel and FSB of the Russian Federation, to name but a few. Chukwuma often says that why he wasn't the one that constructed the FBI headquarters was because the Director had a covert relationship with Gima Nakuto. Well, that has been debunked several times, but who cares… Chukwuma believes it and says it to whoever cares to listen.

One thing that is important to note is that for each project Chukwuma carries out, he often makes use of a secret formula that only the owner of the project knows. Also, because they are buildings that require the best of security systems, he would always construct halls or rooms that had some unimaginable passwords both for entrance and exit. These passwords can't be hacked or reset because they aren't linked to the internet nor are the words found in dictionaries.

Basically, Chukwuma has a pattern of mixing his experiences and coming up with a formula that leads to a password. Someone even insinuated that Chukwuma made use of the birthplace of his second wife's late sister, together with the age of his first wife's brother, all garnished with the birthday of the Chinese President's third son. I mean, it's simply uncrackable, no matter how many times you try. Anyway, he has a secret notebook where he keeps these formulas, completely analogue.

Chika has often visited the construction site to observe the progress of the work there. With time, however, it became a routine for her to visit the place daily, either after dropping Ebuka at school or during her lunch break. And on most of those occasions, Chukwuma was around to show her around and answer her questions.

With her continual visit, Chukwuma soon began developing some affection towards her and Mbe was monitoring. One of the days, Chika needed to report the progress of the work to her superiors. So, that morning she called and went to Chukwuma's office to get the latest updates on the progress of the site. Unknown to her, Mbe had followed her from home to Chukwuma's office.

After she dropped Ebuka at school, she noticed that a navy-blue BMW car that was parked along her street as she left the house was also parked along the way to Ebuka's school. She became curious and asked her driver to change the route he normally takes to the office.

Despite this decision, she observed that a minute after arriving at Chukwuma's office, the same car appeared 100m behind her. She quickly asked the driver to park while she got off. She pretended to get into the office of the architect but followed the next street and walked back. On approaching the position where the BMW waited on the other street, she took out her phone and turned on the video camera to record. But as soon as Mbe saw her, he quickly sped off although Chika was able to capture the plate number of the vehicle.

She went into the architect's office for the scheduled meeting. When she got back to the office that morning, she asked one of her assistants to check the plate number. The result that came in wasn't surprising to her – the vehicle belonged to the FBI. This discovery further reinforced her belief that the FBI or some of its components had something to hide.

***

The fondness for her by Chukwuma increasingly grew. On one of her visits to inspect the site, Chukwuma revealed something to her. It was something that

Chukwuma had only discussed with the Director of National Intelligence and wasn't allowed to discuss it with anyone, including Chika because her security pass doesn't allow her to know of such matters.

But the architect was so much in love with this young mother that he was carried away for a minute. He told her that there's a very important room in an apartment in this building that is currently under furnishing by him. The room will be so special that once you're inside there, no one will ever know that you're there. The room itself doesn't appear on the architectural design of the building, just like some other rooms that are hidden for security purposes seeing that it'll be housing a unit as sensitive as the antiterrorism unit.

In this special room, what appears on the design is just a wall and on the other side are pipes that conduct human excreta to the sewage. Chukwuma added that he and Chika could get in there and do so many things together. He quickly caught himself and asked for pardon. Chika simply giggled and moved on with other questions. After the routine inspection of the place, Chika drove to her office but that secret which the architect divulged kept ringing in her mind.

The week leading to the official opening of the new site, Chika took Ebuka to see the building. Chika has been telling him stories about the new place she'll be moving into the following week and has promised to take him along when the place is finally opened. The building will be officially opened next week, so Chika took Ebuka to see around the place. She wasn't aware of the presence of the architect at the place. When they got there, Chukwuma was excited to see her and especially Ebuka, seeing that he had been itching to see him.

During the mini-tour, Chika introduced her little boy to Chukwuma, who in turn introduced his daughter to Chika. His daughter, Jane is a final year medical student in a neighbouring city and has just returned on holiday to stay with the father.

Jane is the only child of the first wife, who died after a prolonged battle with Hodgkin Lymphoma. The second wife left Chukwuma a year after their wedding because she was fascinated with the lifestyle in Moscow and refused to return. When Chukwuma refused to stay there, Clara, the second wife moved out of his house and went to live with a male friend she had met at the construction site in Moscow. Chukwuma will later discover that they were already courting the months before her departure.

After Chukwuma had introduced Jane to Chika, he quickly adds that Chika and Ebuka should come over for dinner at his place tonight or tomorrow. Chika was reluctant to accept but the facial expression of Jane and the continual insistence of Chukwuma made Chika agree. After taking Ebuka around the building, Chika drove off. Chukwuma and his daughter stayed for a little longer before leaving for his office.

Despite the incident where Mbe was almost caught stalking Chika, he has continued to monitor her moves. This time, not because of the private investigation of

Chika into the death of Ike, but because he noticed the developing affection of Chukwuma towards her, and he was very jealous. He couldn't accept seeing another man have Chika instead of himself. So, during this last inspection of the building before the opening, he came around. Out of jealousy, he had thought of killing the architect but desisted because he didn't want Chika to suspect him seeing she was already investigating the circumstances surrounding Ike's death.

After the mini tour, as Chika drove home with Ebuka; she was a bit disturbed by the presence of Mbe at the site. Mbe had familiarised himself with Chukwuma on a few occasions before now, so his presence at the site wasn't a source of preoccupation for Chukwuma. But Chika knew him better and suspected that his intentions weren't pure.

***

It was evening and Chika was now getting ready to leave for the planned dinner with Chukwuma and his daughter. Ebuka on the other hand couldn't wait for it to get dark; he was itching to go there earlier had his mother let him. He was just so excited about making a new friend or rather discovering an elder sister he doesn't have in Jane, Chukwuma's daughter.

'Mommy, are you not ready yet? Mr Chukwuma said we should come before it's dark,' Ebuka asked Chika.

'Yes, Nnam, I'm ready. And it's just 7 pm; we're not late for the dinner appointment with Mr Chukwuma.' Chika responds.

'Hmmm... yes, but it's good to be on time for appointments Nnem.' Ebuka added.

Chika was a bit shocked when she heard that from Ebuka. I don't mean the issue of punctuality, but that name, Nnem. That's a name she hasn't heard for quite some time now; a name that only one person called her. And this is the first time Ebuka is calling her that. Well, he has called her that a few times in the past, but he was imitating Ikem then as a child.

Chika simply smiled and rubbed her hands around the head of Ebuka. But she couldn't stop thinking about that name because of the memories that come to mind whenever that name enters her ear auricles; it's refreshing, to say the least.

'Nnam, I'm ready. Are you ready?' Chika said smiling.

'Of course, Mom; I was ready before you.' Ebuka wondered while looking at the standing mirror before Chika

'Ok dear, get your jacket, the black leather one I got for you last week, so we can go.'

'Ok, Mom. Let me get it.'

Chika adjusts her slouchy sweater and applies a couple of perfume sprays. She wasn't in for so much preparation; after all, this wasn't dinner with Ikem. She just obliged because of Ebuka and for courtesy as well. So, she just wore a denim skirt, a slouchy sweater, and high boots to match.

***

Chukwuma's house is a cosy bungalow situated a few kilometres outside the city centre. About 10 minutes' drive from Pirro's lane, the environment is neatly and nicely decorated with ornamental plants giving off their fragrances.

As Chika and Ebuka arrived at the house, Jane was already waiting to open the door for them. The ambience was quite breath-taking, courtesy of Jane; with the lightning and other fixtures, Chika felt so welcome. And how about some piece of jazz music in the background? That was simply heavenly.

At the dinner table, they all prayed and went all in *a gustare* the delicacies Jane had graciously prepared for the occasion. While they talked about their lives and the new building, Chukwuma asked Jane and Ebuka to excuse them. He wanted to tell Chika something regarding work that he wouldn't want them to hear. They obliged and went to the living room.

Chukwuma was about to reveal a secret that he's kept for many months, a secret that no one should know. A secret that would jeopardise his life and that of his daughter. A secret that forms the basis for the title of this story, ROOM 39.

CHAPTER 7

The new building was constructed to house the special department of antiterrorism that was formed. It was also going to house CODE RED, a special safe box in one of the rooms that should contain some very highly classified pieces of information. Not even Chika is allowed into that room, let alone that special box.

It is hidden from the original architectural design of the place because the Directors of National Intelligence and FBI wouldn't want anyone to know that the room exists in the first place. Only themselves and whosoever they deem fit is allowed to have the special code for that room and CODE RED.

Chukwuma, the architect, knows. And even before the suggestion came from the Directors, he anticipated that.

He has always constructed special things in all the highly secured edifices he has created. He calls it his golden signature; something that the formal architectural design submitted at the city council doesn't have. But of course, the owners of those buildings know it's there and they always loved it. Call it illegal, call it pride, Chukwuma enjoys his golden signature, and his clients loved the idea even more.

In the construction of this building, however, Chukwuma decided to do something that he has never done before. Something that no one ever suspected. Something that out of pride and a touch of arrogance he wanted to share.

So, one day, he decided to anonymously send an email to a city journalist concerning a puzzle that would fetch 220,000 dollars to anyone who solves it. A puzzle that he was so sure that no one could ever solve, but which if solved would unearth the secret code to Room 39 and Code RED as well.

When the journalist received the anonymous email, he discarded it as spam. After a few months, he received yet another anonymous email with a sentence that seemed to refer to the solution for the puzzle he saw in the previous email. He again trashed it. But when he received the third e-mail a month later at 3am, he thought it was serious and decided to publish it. 'Who knows what this mysterious person wants?'

The journalist is an employee of a local newspaper on Pirro's Lane but unwilling to go through the process of asking permission from his editor, he decided not to publish the puzzle on the pages of the print media (newspaper). He has a personal website where he blogs constantly on certain issues of interest, especially security and politics. So, he decided to attach it as a footnote to his weekly articles.

He runs a weekly electronic newsletter that gives a summary of the socio-political happenings on Pirro for that week. And announcements on major economic events that will take place the following week. So, he decided to add this 'kick' to his articles weekly.

The puzzle soon began to gather many interested people, especially because of the financial reward attached to the solution.

Initially, Kean, the journalist, was reluctant to add the cash reward to it because he wasn't sure if this anonymous email sender would truly send the money. But when Chukwuma agreed to send him 50% of the cash prize, he knew that this game was serious. So, he decided to play along, after all, he got more traffic to his blog, and even if Chukwuma refuses to pay in the end, he could make up for the remaining amount from the paid adverts on his website.

The weekly publication on Kean's blog soon gained wider coverage in the media. Even the local radio station, the print media and other blogs began running articles on the search for the solution to this difficult puzzle. Chukwuma sent an e-mail weekly containing some clues to the journalist who published it on his blog. The radio station and the local newspaper copied from there and made their sales.

So, there were a good number of people who wanted the cash prize. Others were simply curious to resolve this fascinating puzzle. But there was another group that had another objective that goes beyond the cash prize and curiosity. One of such people was a chemical engineer by the name Kachi (Remember Kachi from Chapter One? Yeah)

***

Kachi was a renowned chemical engineering lecturer at the university. He's regarded as one of the best minds that the country has ever produced because of his numerous research work that has been featured in all the most important engineering and biomedical journals.

When the construction of the new building for the antiterrorism unit headed by Chika began, the local newspaper began to investigate what that new building was meant for. There were already the FBI headquarters and the DNI head office as well. Why would they want to construct a separate structure to house an antiterrorism unit? Why not expand an arm of the already existing buildings, instead of destroying the beauty of the city as well as the environment? The City Council had opposed the construction, saying that it was never in the original city plan. But just like the FBI headquarters, the federal government found a way around it.

So, many residents were angry, and the local newspaper began to dig deep into what would happen in this new building. They speculated that there was a specially synthesised drug that the DNI wanted to hide there. That in fact, it was going to be a laboratory for some highly classified experiments of drugs and other chemicals that would be used for their antiterrorism fights. The DNI and FBI refuted that report, but the local newspaper didn't budge and went on to pursue their claims.

***

LET'S GO BACK A LITTLE

Do you remember the corrupt FBI agents that were doing some illegal things with the Collingahs? Yes, Mbe and his team members have been working with the Collingahs, promising them freedom for a huge sum of money. The Collingahs have always cooperated with these men of corrupt minds until something happened.

Mr Collingah senior was nabbed by the FBI some weeks ago at the border when he was trying to escape the country. That caused a rage in his family, and the children felt that Mbe and his men weren't protecting them enough. That they were light men in comparison to the heavy men that ran the Federal Bureau of Investigation.

The first son of Mr Collingah took over the helm of affairs in the family and decided to call it quits with Mbe and his cohorts. Several attempts by Mbe to bury the hatchet proved abortive as Mr Collingah Jr seemed determined to break ties with him and search for another alliance to continue to perpetuate the family's evil business.

The Collingahs were dealers on illegal drugs and child prostitution. They'd import these drugs either by air or water. So, they had men at various ports of entry to allow these drugs into the country. The most wicked part of their business isn't the thousands of lives that get wasted injecting these illegal drugs into their blood vessels or those that inhale the powder form; it was that the children being trafficked were used as human couriers for these drugs.

And there have been multiple cases of children who died out of intoxication because the drugs got released into their systems before they arrived in the country. These are children from rural areas in underdeveloped countries, whose families were promised all sorts of good things if they'd let their children go on this expedition. Sadly, most of them never returned after that.

The Collingahs also ran a luxurious hospitality business, with chains of hotels and restaurants all over the country. As you could imagine, this latter business was a cover-up for their nefarious activities. These young girls 'served' in these hotels and restaurants, and the illegal drugs were also distributed through the same means.

This legal part of the business has for years allowed them to run their 'main' illegal business underground. They made so much more money from illegalities that the legal income from the hotels and restaurants seemed like peanuts in comparison.

Recently, however, the Collingahs decided to enter the nightclub business arena, and because of their client base, the new venture boomed.

One of the major reasons that they decided to get into the nightclub business was because of a new drug that they plan to launch. A psychostimulant that would practically make their competitors run out of business because of how potent it is.

***

Originally meant to be used for chronic pains that have defied opioids, the drug was synthesised by Kachi in one of his laboratories outside the city. Kachi was already working on finding a solution to the chronic pains of neoplastic patients, but his interest in the research grew exceedingly when a venture capitalist approached to finance his project.

He had lost his daughter some years ago to ovarian cancer and that was unimaginably painful for him. After that incident, he decided, together with a few of his assistants, to find a lasting solution to chronic pain. Yes, a drug with some euphoric effect maybe but mostly for the morphine-like effect.

The research work had progressed but at a slow pace because Kachi lacked the necessary financing for it. Not so many investors were willing to invest in that project. The only people that saw a business in what Kachi was working on were the Collingahs.

Mr Collingah already had a bad reputation around the country, so he recruited a venture capitalist to stand in for him to finance the research work. Kachi and his team were completely ignorant of what was going on.

During one of the routine meetings Kachi had with his venture capital, he told them that the research work was going on very well and that soon they'd be able to come up with something that could serve as a preliminary application for clinical trials.

In addition to the above information was a piece of important news. The new chemical (drug) had more euphoric effects than he had earlier thought. It is at least twenty times more potent than heroin, both in the analgesic and euphoric effects it produces. The Venture capitalist seemed visibly excited on hearing this, but Kachi was not.

Kachi had seen the opioid crisis and wouldn't want another drug that would amplify the problem to be pushed into the market or on the streets. So, he told them during the meeting that his team is working hard to see a way to alter the chemical structure of the drug to make it selectively analgesic, with little or no euphoric effects.

The Venture capitalist was enraged and asked him not to do that. That doing such would cut down on his profit.

'No one wanted to invest in this research work because there are many pain relievers already in the market.' He thundered. 'The euphoric effect,' according to him, 'is what cancer patients need most, and it'll make the drug sell everywhere around the world.'

One would think that he was deeply concerned about the pains that cancer patients go through, but he knows what his main objective is. Or rather, what the main objective of his boss, Mr Collingah, is – the euphoric effects of the newly synthesised drug.

Kachi wasn't having it. He told the participants at the meeting that he would go on to synthesise exactly what he had in mind originally, and that no one can stop him, including his financiers. He was willing to source for investment elsewhere if they decided to pull their money. And he reminded them that his contract with them didn't include doing what they were asking.

Needless to say, the meeting ended with the venture capitalist (VC) storming out of the room.

***

One cool morning as Kachi arrived at the laboratory, he noticed some unusual quietness. It's true that he had located this laboratory at the periphery of the city for safety but also for calm and focus, but the silence this morning is so loud that the deaf can hear it. Even a lover of peace and tranquillity like Kachi knew that some noise is better than this tense atmosphere.

As Kachi passed by the few offices at the entrance and walked through the hallway leading to the laboratory, he was shocked at what he saw. The place was completely ransacked, with none of the assistants in view. He couldn't believe what had happened or what was going on. He quickly ran to his office to verify if some sensitive documents he had stored away were still intact.

On reaching his office, he saw his safe box empty. It was at this point that he knew that this wasn't an ordinary accident, and the perpetrators weren't little rats who came to pilfer; the hoodlums knew what they wanted.

Kachi quickly tried to place a call to the local police office to report what he was seeing, but just as he drew his phone out of his briefcase, three huge men appeared from behind and asked him to drop the phone immediately.

At this point, Kachi was visibly shaking, fearing for his life. In a few seconds, his mind ran through a list of the many 'enemies' that could be responsible for such a disaster, but he couldn't figure out who. Not that the list is so long, but none of them could imagine destroying his laboratory and carting away sensitive documents regarding his research work.

Then, just like Apostle Paul in the Bible, who at the prayers of Ananias observed that scales fell from his eye, Kachi's quickly received illumination and the scales fell from his eyes instantly. The list after all isn't that long, it's just one name that is on it – the VC. He recalled how the meeting had ended and the veiled threats he had received in the days following that meeting. But there was still one puzzle left to be solved – why did the VC have to ransack the entire building? Was it necessary? Why cart away the newly synthesised drugs and documents?

So, Kachi mustered up some courage and asked the masked men why the chaos. The response he got wasn't just shocking, it was devastating for Kachi. The response wasn't in words, it was captured in an mp4 format. One of the men drew out a portable device and asked him to watch. It wasn't the explanation that Kachi needed, it wasn't a video that Kachi wanted to ever see whether in this life or the next.

The short video clip that played, with audio, captures a man injecting a dosage of an unknown substance into a lady's arm. The young lady could be seen and heard agonising, pleading that his father helps her out. And the man is seen thinking, running around, trying to reassure her that all will be well. In the end, the man yielded and did what the video says he did. The young lady is Kachi's late daughter, and the man is Kachi.

As Kachi saw the first milliseconds, he screamed in pain and tried to shut down the computer, but the men prevailed upon him. They held his hands and forced him to watch the last minutes of his daughter's death literally. What could be more devastating than this? What other hell can there be that transforms a man into a walking package of agony and misery! He wept as the memories returned.

The Collingahs had succeeded in breaking Kachi. They had taken his drugs, his reserved documents and now this video. For what really? Because he refused to synthesise a drug that produces a euphoric effect twenty times more than heroin. How they obtained that video clip is still unknown, although that was the last thing on Kachi's mind. In fact, Kachi has nothing on his mind; he is blank, drowning in the ocean of agony.

At the end of the video, the men told him that if he ever told the authorities or anyone what had happened to his laboratory and team, they'd make the video public and accuse him of killing the daughter. At that moment, Kachi didn't care if everyone in the world knew what happened. After all, he was dead already.

But as days went by, he advised himself otherwise. He knew that he had a purpose for being alive, although it seems weak and defeated. He wanted to help as many people as possible not to go through what his daughter went through. He wanted to honour the memory of his daughter through his research work, and the mass production of that drug especially. So, going in and out of the court for the rest of his days, and each time being reminded that he was being tried for killing his daughter was the last thing Kachi wanted.

***

Kachi's daughter died of advanced ovarian cancer some years ago. She has been in and out of the hospital for the last 7 years. A trained civil engineer, Nnenna is the only child of Mr Kachi. Kachi's beautiful wife, Uyom died during puerperium (the postpartum period) in a car accident when Nnenna was barely a month old.

One early morning, she was on her way to the hospital for a routine check-up when a drunk driver hit their vehicle. Uyom's driver died on the spot while she sustained a head injury. On getting to the hospital, she was quickly operated on, but the trauma was so severe that she never got out of the coma. She died a few weeks after that. So, Kachi had to raise Nnenna all by himself and that contributed to building a strong bond between the two.

On one of those evenings when Nnenna, his only beloved daughter was crying out of severe pain and begging her father for help, Kachi decided to administer some opioids to her. It was just unbearable seeing his daughter die before him. He had lost his wife in an accident and can't afford to lose the only thing that is keeping him alive.

Seeing his only child suffer is the last thing he could bear. So, he took out a syringe and injected some dose to relieve her of the pain. For a moment Nnenna was fine and smiled, thanking the dad. In a few minutes, she slept off.

Unfortunately, the dosage was so much that the daughter didn't wake up afterwards. The opioid not only sedated her but also caused respiratory depression leading to a complete respiratory arrest. Kachi had lost his world. But what hurts the most was that he 'killed' her.

How these evil men got the video is just beyond him. He knew that he had installed cameras in his house since the birth of Nnenna, but how these hoodlums were able to lay their hands on the tape is indecipherable. But he wasn't even bothered about the video anymore. The memories of his multiple losses just came back haunting him. The weight of the things he did and did not do came suddenly on him. Kachi couldn't help but scream in pain. They had touched his weak point and he was visibly paralysed.

The drugs were gone and so were his years of labour too. Kachi was left with nothing but death and maybe… just maybe his teaching career. Because once the video goes public, his teaching career will also bid him farewell.

Not wanting to be arrested for the death of his daughter, Kachi decided to leave the city for a while. To metabolise his losses and know what next horrible experience life reserved for him. The entire university community was shocked when they heard some months later that Kachi is now a schoolteacher in one of the secondary schools in a distant rural area several kilometres away from town.

***

Mbe is still at daggers drawn with the new heir apparent of the Collingah empire after Mr Collingah Sr was arrested. So, one of the days, he learnt that the Collingahs were keeping some drugs which they wanted to produce en masse for use in their nightclubs. He decided to hatch a plan with his team on how to steal the drugs and use them to extort money from the Collingahs. Unfortunately for him, the store, just like the entire compound, is constantly guarded by armed men that work for the Collingahs. So, Mbe couldn't access the room where the drugs are stored.

After a month from the incident at Kachi's laboratory, the Collingahs decided to set up a new laboratory in a distant city. The aim was to start mass production seeing that the launch of their nightclub business was a few weeks away. They have found a new team of chemists, and together with the research documents and the original drugs Kachi had synthesised, they were set to increase, multiply and replenish the entire country. Once the new drugs hit the nightclubs, hotels, and restaurants, they were sure to rake in money in millions per night.

So, they decided to convey the drugs out of the safe storage in the house to this new laboratory. When Mbe learnt of the move, he agreed with his team to steal the drugs along the way.

So, on the day of the movement, Mbe with his team waylaid the transporters, killed the security men guarding them and carted away the drugs and all the relevant documents that they could lay hands on.

While running away, they decided to stop by an uncompleted building to plan their next move. When they got to there, they all agreed that the drugs needed to be kept in a safe place together with the documents. They wanted a lot of money from the Collingahs for the stolen items and were not willing to negotiate otherwise.

As none of their houses seemed safe for such storage, Mbe suggested that the items be kept in the new building under construction for the antiterrorism unit. The construction of the building was almost done, but it hadn't opened yet. The official opening is in a few weeks, so they decided to keep the stolen items there, collect money from the Collingahs and then come back to get the drugs and documents. So, they'd have either gotten the money they wanted from the Collingahs, or they'd find a better place to keep them.

**

That evening, Mbe drove to Chukwuma's office with one of his team members and asked Chukwuma to show them the safest place in the building. When Chukwuma asked to know why, they responded that it was an order from the FBI Director, and it should be treated as an emergency.

Chukwuma quickly took the items from them and asked them to wait behind while he went in alone. Mbe initially refused but after much argument, he gave in.

Chukwuma went inside, making sure he was not followed by anyone. He finds his way to Room 39, and deposits the items into Code RED. He quickly closed the place and came out to bid the men goodbye.

CHAPTER 8

So, when Jane and Ebuka left, Chukwuma decided to unveil the secrets of the building to Chika. He began by telling Chika patches of stories of the jobs he's done in various countries and the names he gave to each of the buildings he's constructed. Chika didn't know exactly why he was telling the story of his life basically, but since it sounded interesting, she listened carefully. Moreover, the meals that Jane had prepared for the dinner were quite delicious. Who doesn't love the taste of pasta alla carbonara, lo spiedino served with a beautiful ceramic, a cup of wine, all under an atmosphere that is cosy, exclusive and with a touch of ancient feel to it?

Unknown to Chika however, Chukwuma was gradually telling her the pieces of the puzzle he's been releasing to the journalist via email, although in a non-sequential manner. She had read of the rave on the local newspapers and blog about some strange puzzle that people were attempting to solve, but she had never been that interested in digging deep.

As the conversation progressed, Chika began to observe a pattern in the stories that Chukwuma was telling. A pattern she wasn't aware of what it served but which she decided to however follow, peradventure Chukwuma asks questions at the end of the stories to test her comprehension abilities. It was as she did this that she observed that the initials of all the countries Chukwuma mentioned, when pieced together would give the name CABIOJINIA. Cabiojinia is the man that decorated the DNI headquarters on Pirro's Lane.

But she didn't know what it was for. 'What's the relationship between Chukwuma and Cabiojinia?' she asked herself. She wanted to find out from Chukwuma, but she preferred not to interrupt him, waiting for the stories to end and her turn to speak. Moreover, Chukwuma may be telling stories that have no deeper meaning to them. So, she didn't want to sound awkward.

Then, at one point, Chukwuma dropped his cutleries, wiped his mouth, and adjusted his chair as if he was about to say something very important. At this point, Chika was more attentive, although she pretended to be more involved in munching her meat than in the stories that Chukwuma told. He told her that there is a special room inside the new Antiterrorism building called Room number 39. It is called Room 39 not because it's the 39th room in the building; it's a highly secured apartment that doesn't appear in the official design that was submitted to the department of Urban development. That official copy is accessible to the public at the local government headquarters. So, this secured fortress was purposely cropped out of the public design.

ROOM 39

39 however represents the secret code for gaining access into this special apartment in the building. The first door asks for the secret code, the second door has a fingerprint sensor, and the last door scans the iris before you'll be granted access to the safest place in the apartment. All these will be activated on the day the building will be handed over to the DNI. For now, only the security code of the first door is active.

The code 39 isn't in English, but in Igbo language – IRI ATO NA ITOOLU. Once inside the apartment, the exit code is different as well. But Chukwuma said that he won't tell the exit code to anyone until when the building officially opens, and he hands the keys over to her and the Directors of the FBI and DNI. The exit code, he added, changes every 30 seconds, so once in there, you need to be quick whenever you want to exit.

***

Kachi has continued to teach in his new secondary school. He fled the city to escape arrest because the Collingahs threatened to make the video of his daughter's death public.

One day Kachi was on his way to school when a newspaper front page caught his attention. He had heard of the construction work going on but hadn't been interested in knowing for what reason and why it seemed to raise much clamour. So, whenever he saw that the front page of the newspapers was on the said building, he'd simply leave buying them completely.

But today was different. Aside from the bold title on the building project, there was also a cover story on the new drug that the Collingahs seem to be trying to distribute. The newspaper had gotten information from an anonymous source that the Collingahs were going into the entertainment business as a cover-up to flood the nightclubs with this new pill.

When Kachi read the headings of the newspaper, he immediately knew that this would interest him. So, on alighting the bus, he quickly bought the newspaper. Also on the front page was a title, though minuscule, concerning the puzzle that everyone except him was talking about. So, in one Daily, he had the latest information regarding the building, the puzzle and, most importantly, the new drug in town.

Well, he was more interested in the drug and vowed to himself that he would do anything in his power to stop its distribution. He also learned that the Collingahs seemed to have lost possession of the drug they had stolen from his laboratory and were searching for ways to recover it.

His curiosity led him to start solving the puzzle, but the more he did, the more he figured that the three items that he read in the newspaper could all be linked – the building, the puzzle and the drug were all pointing in the same direction. It was a fascinating mix that Kachi didn't want to miss. So, he set out on a mission to unravel the whole puzzle and lay his hands on those pills.

***

After the theft orchestrated by Mbe and his team, the Collingahs didn't spend much time discovering who was responsible. After all, they knew the man that was interested in getting them either jailed or extorting huge sums of money from them. But they couldn't fathom how Mbe was able to get the secret info regarding the transportation of the drugs. The important documents that the security guards transported included all the formulae of that drug and the steps involved in its synthesis. The Collingahs wanted both because the new chemists and biologists they employed needed both the samples of the drug and the formulae that Kachi had painstakingly written down.

So, they quickly devised a means to hunt down Mbe and his men. They were to kidnap all the cohorts of Mbe and their families until Mbe gets them those drugs and documents. Instructions soon got to all the security agents working for the Collingahs, and the search began. The agents had clear instructions not to kill any of the men, but to take down any member of their family if that would make Mbe's team succumb. And if these men tried to escape, well....

When Mbe learnt that some of his men and their families had been kidnapped, he quickly made plans to fly his family out of the country. He knew that the entire city and indeed the entire country was unsafe for his wife and children. The Collingahs had their agents all over the country, and where they didn't have, they'd recruit local mercenaries to do their evil bidding. Mbe knew this, after all, he was under the pay of this deadly family until a few months ago.

On this unfortunate day, Mbe had arranged with a private jet owner, who was his friend, to fly his family out of the country. He didn't want to book seats in a commercial airline and go through the normal controls at the airport. No one knows where these Collingahs are lurking, and they might disguise themselves as airport workers to carry out their nefarious activities. The illegal business of the Collingahs majorly travelled by air, so to think that they don't have men among the airport personnel, including pilots, would be infantile.

Unfortunately for Mbe, one of his men that was captured told the Collingahs Mbe's plan to whisk his family away from the country via air. So, the Collingahs quickly contacted their mercenaries at the major airports and told them to be on the lookout for Mbe and his family.

***

Mbe arrived at the airport in a regular taxicab with his family, disguised in blue jeans, a white t-shirt, and a cap. His family all dressed in a simple manner with face masks. They briskly go through the normal checks with no hassles and walk down to meet Mbe's friend – the owner of the private jet.

Mbe felt that something was wrong with how peaceful the whole process went; no suspicious moves around the airport and no curious eyes when they passed through the gate. Everything went too smoothly to be true. And no flight attendant to welcome them aboard the private jet. He knew the exact private jet that belonged to his friend, but he was expecting that his friend would send one of his attendants to meet with them.

While he was still lost in his thoughts, he noticed the flight door open and a man walking down the airstairs. He looked like his friend and for a moment he could heave a sigh of relief; he could see a light at the end of this very dark tunnel. He beamed with smiles as he approached his friend to exchange greetings. But as they climbed the boarding stairs, Mbe's greatest fears seem to return suddenly. He wondered why the friend was at the airport at that time. He had told him a few hours ago that he would be in a business meeting at the time of Mbe's proposed travel. Also, he won't be travelling for the next two weeks.

"How come he's at the airport waiting for us?" Mbe thought to himself. And just in the middle of the airstairs, Mbe had a change of mind. He sensed danger; someone has betrayed his trust. He doesn't know what the deal was, but he was sure his friend had sold him to the Collingahs.

Mbe quickly turns and asks his family to drop their luggage and run back to the airport terminal. But just as the words escaped his mouth, two men emerged from the passenger boarding bridge walking towards them. From their look and gait, he knew who they were and what their mission was. As he turned to see if they could run inside the aircraft, two mercenaries stood on both sides of the door of the aircraft. Mbe knew that his end was close. His family was ushered inside the aeroplane by the two agents at the door, while the other two escorted Mbe to a limousine parked a few metres away.

As Mbe got into the limousine, he got the shocker of his life. Mr Collingah Sr had in some mysterious way escaped from the prison. Mbe didn't know how or when, but he certainly knew that Mr Collingah didn't serve his term in jail. He was also aware that neither himself nor his team is relevant to Mr Collingah Sr anymore. If he could get out of prison without them, he certainly had connections that go way up above Mbe and his men.

Sitting beside Mr Collingah Sr at the back seat of the limousine was his son who had been running the entire Collingahs' empire while his father was in jail. There wasn't any exchange of pleasantries when they saw Mbe.

As Mbe entered the limousine, the driver immediately drove away. When they got to the point where Mbe had waylaid the security guards that transported the drugs, the driver stopped and asked Mbe to get out of the car. As he opened the door, Mr Collingah Jr told him that he had three days to return the drugs and all the documents or lose his family forever. As Mbe got out of the car, the driver quickly drove away.

When Mbe got out of the car, he quickly ran home to plot strategies on how to rescue his wife and kids. He knew that the Collingahs desperately needed these drugs and especially those documents. He didn't know how important those items were to the Collingahs, but he knew that whatever made them that desperate, to the point of kidnapping his family, and warranted the appearance of both Collingah Sr and Jr in that limousine, meant life or death to them. So, he decided to change the game, to dictate the tune with those priceless possessions in his custody.

He quickly called two of his friends and told them that he planned to use those items against the Collingahs. He was convinced they weren't going to harm his family until they had laid their hands on the drugs and documents. Three days were enough for him to visit Chukwuma and get the items, but he delayed purposely to know what the next move of the Collingahs would be.

***

Two days have passed since that threat was made and Mbe has refused to contact them. He hasn't contacted Chukwuma either to get the drugs and documents out of the safe box in the new antiterrorism building where he hid them. In Mbe's opinion, it's best to leave the drugs and documents there until he was sure of the release of his family and colleagues, with a huge sum of money in recompense.

Well, Mbe was making a big mistake. It is true that the Collingahs desperately needed those items, especially the documents, but one thing Mbe didn't realise was that the Collingahs weren't ready for any negotiations this time. They were not ready to do any further business with Mbe and his team. All they wanted were those items and they were ready to kill just to lay their hands on the stolen items. They wanted Mbe and his cohorts to return the items with no delays, else they'd come after them and their families till the last man is dead.

When the third day arrived and Mbe wasn't forthcoming with the items, the Collingahs called him and gave him an hour to deliver, or they'd kill one of his children in front of his wife. Mbe pretended not to understand the weight of the threat, but rather threatened to expose them to the public. He vowed to go to the news media and expose all their dirty activities, with highly indicting documents and video clips. That threat further infuriated the Collingahs, and at 6pm that evening Mbe received a shocking video message.

He was with his friends in an abandoned warehouse planning on how to rescue his family and the other colleagues that were kidnapped by the Collingahs when the video message came in. The sender was from the camp of the Collingahs. Mbe quickly signalled one of his men to open the message so they could know what the Collingahs were up to.

As the video played, the images that were displayed were horrifying, to say the least. Everyone in the hall was shocked and for the first time they knew that the Collingahs had no limits to what they were willing to do to get those stolen items back

The video clip showed Mbe's teenage daughter sexually abused on video by Mr Collingahs' men until she passed out. Everyone in the hall was petrified for long minutes after the video clip had ended. Mbe didn't know what nor how to feel. He was both raging inside and feeling very cold outside. He's an evil man but he's never done nor thought of going this far in his evildoings. What was more alarming was when the voice of Mr Collingah subtly came up at the end of the video saying, "Mbe, guess who's next?" and the camera pans to the right, showing the marred visage of Mbe's wife.

After seeing the video, Mbe's countenance changed. His plans have been shattered by what he saw. He now knows that the Collingahs were not disposed to negotiate at all. They were ready to rape and kill his wife and children and still come after him and the drugs. Mbe was furious and for a moment thought of driving straight to the Collingahs compound and shooting everyone. But he knew that would mean the end of his entire family and himself. So, he resolved rather to do what the Collingahs always asked for – deliver the drugs and documents and get his family back.

***

It was now around 7.30pm the third day when Mbe decided to yield to the demands of the Collingahs. So, he quickly drove to Chukwuma's office that evening to collect the drugs and documents that Chukwuma was asked to keep some weeks ago. Mr Chukwuma often closes from work at 6pm. But today he stayed longer because he had some foreign visitors who had come to discuss a new project they were embarking on. He was done with the construction of the new Antiterrorism Unit's building and so was free to take up another major project in another part of the country or even outside the country.

When Mbe arrived at his office at 7:40pm, Chukwuma had closed from the office and was walking towards his car. Mbe hurriedly drove towards him and got out of his car to meet with him.

'Please, I need those items we gave to you to keep for us a few weeks ago. I need them now.' Mbe said.

'Excuse me. Do you need those items now?' Chukwuma asked, shaking his head in confusing surprise.

'Yes, I do. I need them now. Right now.' Mbe's voice was shaky as if he was about to cry. But also, desperate.

'But it's late already. Why do you need them now?' Chukwuma questioned.

'How is that your business?! We gave you the items to keep for us and now we need them. Simple!' Mbe's desperation was now growing more visible.

'But you also told me that it was the FBI Director that asked you to keep the items in a safe place here. How is it that he suddenly needs them at this time of the night?' Chukwuma further probed. It was unbelievable that the FBI Director would make such a request at almost 8pm, without prior notice. So, Chukwuma seemed suspicious of the whole thing.

'What the hell is wrong with you?! We gave you items from the FBI Director and the Director needs them now! Is that too hard to comprehend? Go inside there and get me those drugs immediately!' Mbe shouted.

'Drugs?! What the hell are you talking about? Drugs? Did you give me drugs to keep for you?' Chukwuma said bewildered. He seemed completely lost, as the conversation was sounding more and more strange to him. First Mbe shows up at his office to hide some items from the FBI Director with no prior notice, and that very hurriedly. Then, the same Mbe shows up at night to collect the said items, still with no prior information from the FBI Director. And now he learns that the said item is illegal drugs. The entire conversation was getting weird, and Chukwuma doesn't have 'weird conversation' on his to-do list that night.

"So, you mean that the items you gave me to keep for you in the safe box of this building meant for the Antiterrorism Unit are illegal drugs?" Chukwuma questioned further.

"Yes, drugs man! We gave you some drugs and documents to keep in that hell of a safe house or room or whatever you call it. Now we need them. Just go in there, get me the items – the drugs and documents – and we'll be fine." Mbe said, reaching for his gun.

At this point, Chukwuma didn't know what else to do. Should he refuse to give to Mbe the sensitive items that he isn't sure the FBI Director had asked him to bring, or should he just give the items to Mbe and walk home, then act as if nothing happened? He pondered.

While he pondered, Mbe's voice roared again "Get the hell in there and get me those items, or I'll kill you here and go in there to take them myself. I missed you the last time and I'm certainly not going to miss you today if you fail to give me those items. You've been messing around with a lady that I love, and I've kept my cool. If you don't get me those drugs and documents now, I promise that you, your daughter, and everyone you love won't see the dawn. We know where you live, what you do daily, and all the people related to you."

Chukwuma didn't initially understand what Mbe meant by "I missed you the last time." But his mind quickly flashed back to a couple of weeks ago when he was being trailed by a dark vehicle close to his avenue. The vehicle had followed him from around his office to the entrance of his avenue. He recalls that it was after a police van passed that the vehicle trailing him disappeared.

That was Mbe. After his attempt to woo Chika failed, he continued to stalk her. And lately, he has grown increasingly jealous of the relationship between Chukwuma and Chika and was determined to stop it using any means possible. The said night he trailed Chukwuma intending to threaten him in front of his daughter. And if Chukwuma insisted on continuing the relationship with Chika, he wouldn't hesitate to shoot him.

CHAPTER 9

A t this point Chukwuma knew that Mbe wasn't only serious – he could tell that from his voice – but there was no way he was going home tonight alive. Mbe just confessed to attempted murder, stealing drugs and other vital items from the Collingahs, and worst still, Mbe's face was in full glare. So, there was no way an astute FBI agent like Mbe would allow him to go free. He figured that Mbe just wants to lay his hands on the drugs and documents and then proceed to kill him.

So, Chukwuma opted to die instead, after all, he was dead the day he began to take interest in Chika and was buried the day he accepted to take those items into Room 39. The case was closed from the beginning. At this point, he decided to find a way of escape and if that didn't work, he wouldn't give Mbe the drugs either.

"You can't get into that safe room at this time. Why not come here early tomorrow morning and I'll give everything to you. No one is going to know anything that happened." Chukwuma insisted.

"You think I'm stupid, right? I'll simply laugh, shake your hands and let you go, right?" Mbe beams his evil laughter

"I don't think you're stupid. Not at all. But Room 39 is a very specialised room that has several protocols for going in and out. If I attempt bridging any of those protocols, in the next couple of minutes, we'll have all the security apparatus surrounding this building. A signal will be sent to all of them that someone is trying to bridge the security protocols of the safe room." Chukwuma continued.

"That's hogwash. You projected and constructed this hell of a building. There must be a way to get in and get out without triggering the alarms. You can't fool me. Get on man, I have no time to waste!" Mbe furiously shuts him up.

Chukwuma reluctantly walks back to the building to open it. As he gets inside the building, they both walk across the offices leading to Room 39. Mbe couldn't believe his eyes as he saw the sophistication in the building; it was an intricate construction, like a labyrinth that only a mathematics genius like Chukwuma could come up with.

They continued to walk to the side of the building where Room 39 is. Chukwuma was in front, while Mbe followed closely at gunpoint.

While they talked, Chukwuma slowly opened the first entrance to Room 39 and walked in. Then, he triggered the silent alarm by the door. Mbe didn't notice that initially, but when he saw a red-light blinking, he knew that something fishy was going on. Chukwuma on his part was aware that if Mbe steps his feet inside Room 39, there was no way Mbe could leave the room without him given the security measures in place. It was either Mbe spared the life of Chukwuma till they were out of the building with the drugs and documents, or he can kill Chukwuma and leave without the items.

"What the hell did you just do? You set off the alarm?" Mbe fumed in rage.

"I told you that if I bridged the security protocols, the alarm would go off. I told you." Chukwuma seems to become unusually bold and that confuses Mbe.

"And I told you that if you did that you'd die, together with your daughter and everyone you love. How stupid can you be – you lose the drugs, documents and still lose your life and family." Mbe retorted.

"Ahahaha… ahahaha… Do you think that you're the only one who can play this game? Well, let me educate you. My daughter will be out of this country in the next 3 minutes, sorry 30 seconds. I sent her a message the moment I sensed your threat towards my family. Come on! Do you think that a man like me who has constructed highly secured buildings for the Mossad, the Arab security apparati and the FSB won't know a thing or two about security? Do you think I got to this level just by knowing how to erect nice buildings? Chukwuma said, mocking Mbe.

"Shut the hell up and get me the items now! I don't care who you are or what you have done in the past. Get me those drugs and documents immediately." Mbe thunders.

"How dumb can you be? And by the way, the night you trailed me to my house, you got saved by the police vehicle. I was ready to take good care of you had you come closer. But as I said, the police vehicle helped you that day." Chukwuma continues.

"It doesn't matter to me. You're dead to me anyway. Your daughter can run to anywhere for all I care, but I'm going to find her." Mbe tries to project courage, although his voice portrays fear and desperation.

"Granted, you caught me off guard tonight. I wasn't expecting you, so I wasn't with any of my ammunition. But also, you are a coward because you won't drop your gun and fight with your hands. That's ok. You've won tonight, and I lost. But to think that I'll allow you Coward to harm my daughter… that's stupid. Yes, you are both stupid and a coward.' Chukwuma said.

As he said these words, Mbe grew increasingly angry. While he thought of killing Chukwuma, he was also aware that he desperately needed the drugs to save his family from the Collingahs. But to do the latter, he needs to go into Room 39 with Chukwuma alive and leave the Room with him alive too. And while he's at it, the security operatives may arrive, and he'd lose everything. Mbe was confused. He didn't know what decision to take.

"You can come to get the drugs, or you can escape for your life. Those are the only two options you have, coward. You can't have both. Your choice coward!" Chukwuma shouted.

At this point, Mbe lost it and emptied his barrel on Chukwuma. "To hell with you and the drugs!" he screamed as he fatally shot Chukwuma. Mbe quickly runs back, following the path they had walked. He narrowly escapes before the police could arrive at the building.

***

When Chukwuma triggered the alarm, all the security apparati were immediately alerted. So, some police officers and FBI agents were immediately deployed to the new Antiterrorism headquarters to ascertain what the problem was. Unfortunately, before they could arrive at the crime scene, Mbe had escaped leaving no traces at all.

As Mbe escaped from the building, he quickly called his FBI friends to notify them of what had happened. He was aware that some FBI personnel would be assigned to the scene of the crime and so asked his friends to intercept whoever was assigned and replace them.

Mbe was also very certain that the security cameras in the building must have captured him at some point. On entering the building with Chukwuma, he had wittingly flipped a hoodie over his head and worn a pair of dark goggles to disguise. But he was still certain that in the long run, with the postural and gait analysis that the Attorney's office would conduct, it won't be long until he's uncovered.

As he drove for a few metres away from the building, he quickly turned when he learnt that his friends were on their way to the building. On reaching the building, their first aim is to quickly go to the control room and extract the tape recorder. Then, delete the file recording for that hour and insert it back into the system. The second aim is to go into room 39 and get the stolen drugs and documents before the police officers would find out. So, Mbe quickly asked them to divide themselves into two groups. He would lead the group that goes to the control room, while the other group goes to recover the stolen items.

The FBI agents were the first to arrive at the crime scene because Mbe had tipped them off. Mbe quickly moves to the control room on the first floor. At first, they were lost, not knowing the exact location of the control room. But having visited the building a few times, he was able to locate it. They quickly extracted the tape, inserted it into their system and performed a complete reset of the tape. While they did so, they were on the lookout for when the police and other security operatives would arrive at the building.

On reaching the place where the lifeless body of Chukwuma lay, the corrupt agents tried to enter Room 39 but discovered that the entrance was shut. The security door had locked 30 seconds after Chukwuma was shot. Chukwuma had hoped to enter the Room and quickly activate the automatic lock. But Mbe was at a close range, so that wasn't possible. When the corrupt agents asked Mbe for the code, he told them that he doesn't know since he stayed a distance from Chukwuma.

As they sought a way to break into Room 39, the police and another group of FBI agents arrived at the building. When they questioned how Mbe and his friends arrived so early, Mbe simply answered that they were within the neighbourhood for a covert operation when they observed some strange movements around the building. So, they quickly rushed to the scene. And on why they were on the first floor where the control room is, they said that they were searching for the gunman, peradventure he was still hiding in the building.

Afraid of being unmasked, Mbe and his friends decided to leave the scene after they made sure that any evidence that would link them to the death of Chukwuma was tampered with. They left with the excuse that since other FBI agents had arrived at the crime scene, that they will now take their leave to continue the covert operation they were assigned to do in the vicinity.

***

Chika was at the dinner table with Ebuka and her parents when she received a call informing her that Chukwuma was dead. She was in utter shock and disbelief. When she inquired and learnt that he was shot, she was more confused. She didn't know Chukwuma as someone who had enemies around the country. He was an easy-going person who seemed to get along with everyone around the world... with no prejudice, just projects and money. Nothing more.

She excuses herself and drives quickly to the crime scene to see things for herself. On reaching the scene, Chukwuma's body had already been taken to the Attorney General's office for forensic investigation. She asks the investigators some questions regarding the crime scene, and they give her the few details they had.

The whole thing was still shocking to Chika. She quickly puts a call through to Jane's line to know if she was home and safe. But her line was unreachable, so Chika decided to drive to Chukwuma's house. A few metres away from his house, he saw three men quickly enter a car and speed off. She slowly stops her car, parks by the side, and turns off her car lights.

As they drove past her, she took photos of the vehicle. When she was sure that they were gone, she ignited her engine and drove to Chukwuma's house to inspect what was happening. On reaching the house, she observes that the lights are off and there seems to be no movement inside. She goes around the building, takes some photos, and calmly drives away. She was determined to know what happened to Chukwuma and the whereabouts of his daughter. And no one would be able to stop her this time.

ROOM 39

PART THREE

Only a genius could do this

ROOM 39

CHAPTER 10

The following day when Chika came to the office, the DNI organised a meeting during which an investigative body was set up to examine what led to Chukwuma's death and who was or were responsible. Chika was expecting to head the committee given that the new building was meant to house her unit, and she is the most senior person in the antiterrorism squad since her recent promotion as the director of the unit.

The most surprising thing, however, is that she was asked not to participate in any shape or form throughout the process of the investigation; she was not to ask any of the members questions regarding the investigation nor suggest any path she thinks they should investigate. According to the DNI Director, there were other important developments that the agency wanted her to focus on. She could go on with her role as the Director of the Unit. Chika was very upset with him and with everyone that took such a senseless decision.

After the meeting, Chika asked to meet with the Director. When she entered his office, the DNI director was already set with his answer. As Chika began to pour out her frustration over the decision to exclude her from the investigation committee, the director was unmoved. When she was done, he told her that her relationship with Chukwuma is the main reason why she was being excluded from the committee. He doesn't want her to be emotionally involved in the investigation.

He told her that he learnt that she visited Chukwuma's house last night after the incident, and that approach without following due process was unacceptable. All of Chika's plea fell on deaf ears, as the director was bent on leaving her out of the entire process, not because she's a suspect, but because she would lack objectivity in her approach.

***

Two weeks ago, while the new building was at its final phase, the DNI Director called Chika to have some progress reports. Chika gave him updates on how everything was going and told him that the building would be completed earlier than the scheduled opening date.

While Chika spoke, the Director nodded and asked very few questions, unlike the other times when they had met for progress reports. Chika wasn't comfortable with his cold attitude and desired to know if anything was the matter. After multiple trials, the Director told her that there were reports of her affair with Chukwuma. Chika tried to refute them, asking the Director to treat them as rumours, because that is what they are. She acknowledged seeing Chukwuma a few times outside his office, but even then, they were strictly official meetings except for a dinner appointment they had with their family present. Moreover, she wasn't over the death of Ikem yet; 'it'd be insulting to Ikem's memory to go after another man now, while investigations into his death are still ongoing, although very slowly,' she added.

What the Director doesn't know is that Chika hasn't given up on her quest to unravel the behind-the-scenes of Ike's death. All she is doing, both with her office and her relationship with Chukwuma, is to find useful information that would help her uncover the truth behind Ike's supposed accident. To date, no one has found his body despite numerous searches in the said river.

Chukwuma and indeed others may have thought that Chika was increasingly growing fond of him, but those were mere illusions. What Chukwuma was seeing were projections of his mind, as far as Chika was concerned. However, Chika liked his personality, and even if she didn't get any leads from Chukwuma in the end, she still wants to maintain a cordial relationship with his family, especially with the daughter Jane, a truly fantastic young lady that loves Chika's son, Ebuka, as her little brother.

After her explanations, the Director asked her to be very careful with her relationship with Chukwuma, as such an intimate relationship may pose a threat to national security given the secret information that Chika is privy to. She nodded in agreement and since then further reduced her conversations with Chukwuma.

***

Chika wouldn't listen to being kept out of the investigation. She doesn't understand why the DNI

Director would exclude her from such an important case given her new role as director of the Antiterrorism unit.

'Am I one of the suspects because of my relationship with Chukwuma? Is Chukwuma's death in some way linked to the death of Ikem? Could the murderer be the same person that killed Ikem? What are they trying to cover up?' were some of the questions that kept racing through Chika's mind. Whatever the answers were, she perceived that something was fishy about the whole incident.

The security operatives she met at the crime scene hadn't many details to give to her. When she attempted contacting the Attorney General's office to have access to the forensic report, her request was denied. All of these made Chika desire to unearth the truth behind these two high profile murders – she considers Ikem's death as murder. So, besides the death of Ikem, Chika was determined to know who killed Chukwuma, and she was willing to go to any length on her own.

***

When she drove home that day, she decided to confide in her father Dede. All the while, her father had observed how she reacted whenever the discussion of Ike's death came up. She would always disbelieve the account of his death to a point that everyone around felt she's a bit mentally unstable. But her father, being a veteran, shared the same opinion as herself, although he kept his thoughts to himself.

So, when Chika began talking about the gruesome murder of Chukwuma, her father paid close attention.

She explained how her relationship with Chukwuma was purely professional, although Chukwuma wanted more. For her, she wanted to see if Chukwuma would help with some information regarding Ike's death seeing how close he was to the FBI Director. She also explained how the DNI is completely excluding her from the investigation into Chukwuma's death, citing unfounded allegations of an amorous relationship between her and Chukwuma.

After the explanations, Chika decided to intimate the father of her plans to proceed with the investigation privately. She has been investigating the death of Ike and believes there's some connection between the two cases, although she can't concretely point at how and where.

The father assures Chika that he would protect her little boy Ebuka and Chika's mom if Chika decided to take some time off to run a private investigation. That he was willing to sacrifice his life for theirs, after all, despite his sacrifice for the country, the country didn't reward him as much. The only things he had left are Chika, Ebuka and his wife. And he would fight to know who killed his son-in-law.

The next day, Chika got to the office quite early to do her normal duties. But she intended to finish early and visit the site of the incident. So, when she was done with her office duties, she drove to the new building. On reaching the crime scene, she met with some investigators who to a great extent kept their findings secret seeing they were instructed to report only to the Directors of the DNI and FBI. When they told her that no arrests were made yet and there was no one on the list of most wanted people, she was confused.

'The new building was meant to house the Antiterrorism Unit of the nation. It has all the security fitting in place to make it impossible for anyone to escape without leaving a fingerprint, footprint, video image or any other form of evidence.' She thought to herself. 'If Chukwuma was killed inside room 39, and the security officers arrived at the scene almost immediately, how did the killer escape the building in the first place? And how was it possible for the security cameras not to have captured him?' she kept musing as she walked around the building. 'Or could it be that the killer is actually among the security officers that came that night to the crime scene?' She continued.

Mbe and his men had left the crime scene the night of Chukwuma's assassination before Chika arrived, so she couldn't tell if they were there or not. So, Chika asked the investigators to tell her the names of all the people that came that night to the crime scene and at what time each arrived. The investigators declined her request citing the same reasons the DNI Director had given the day of the committee's constitution. Chika got offended with them and left the building.

One of the people in the committee that was set up by the DNI to investigate the death of Chukwuma was Chika's junior colleague in the antiterrorism unit. So, after the incident at the crime scene, Chika contacted him privately and asked for some information regarding their investigations. He refused to talk over the phone and instead preferred a physical meeting at night in one of the restaurants in a neighbouring city. He knows how sensitive the investigation is and was aware that his phone was being monitored just like those of all the members of the committee.

Chika continued to visit the crime scene repeatedly, ignoring the warnings of the DNI Director. On one of those occasions, she observed a dark blue Ford vehicle trailing her. Mbe's team observed that Chika was getting more and more interested in the case and was afraid that she might see something incriminating. Initially, they thought to kill her, but Mbe refused, preferring rather to trail her, peradventure she's able to get into the building and help them recover the stolen items that Chukwuma kept inside Room 39.

One of the afternoons when Chika left her office for lunch, one of the members of Mbe's team sneaked into her office and hid a tiny electronic device in her jacket. Seeing that Chika's office is constantly checked for security purposes, Mbe thought to hide the microphone on her clothing. That way they're able to both hear her conversations inside and outside the office whenever she wears that jacket. They'd also be able to monitor her exact location whenever she has that jacket with her. It was a better option than having the device affixed to the curtain in her office or on the back of Ike's picture frame on her desk.

***

The FBI and the DNI decided to uncover the secret code of Room 39. Chukwuma had refused to release both the entrance and exit codes until the building was completed and handed over to them. According to him, it is a policy he has maintained since his first construction of a building for a security outfit.

In fact, it was well spelt out in the contract he signed with them that no one would ask for the security codes until the day of the handover. Chukwuma had planned to release the entrance code and the combinations for the exit code to Chika and the Directors a night before handing the building over to them.

When the DNI observed that Chika went on with a private investigation despite warnings from her director, she was suspended from the agency until the investigation into the death of Chukwuma is concluded. The Director gently asked her to go for paid therapy leave because she looked mentally drained and unstable. They'd call her back in a couple of months when the entire drama is over.

Although that would deprive Chika access to certain privileges she enjoys, and the possibility of getting vital pieces of information from people around, she thought it was an opportunity to focus her attention on these two fronts wholly. Several times in the past days, the Director had sought ways to keep her occupied with minor cases of acts of terrorism across the globe. Although she loves her work and considers every act of terror important, she felt this wasn't the time to pin her down with things junior colleagues could handle. So, the suspension came as a relief for her.

Chika has made repeated attempts to see the body of Chukwuma but to no avail. She wanted to examine his wounds and the bullets that were extracted from his body seeing that the reports talked about shooting. With the bullets, she can trace the manufacturer, the type of gun used, and maybe the killer. She also wanted to know if there were any signs of physical altercation before his death, maybe the fingerprint of the murderer might show on Chukwuma's body.

Seeing the impossibility of gaining access to Chukwuma's body, Chika decided to speak with her source once more. Maybe the committee has analysed the pieces of evidence found at the building site and understands what happened. This time, however, Chika's source couldn't say much because according to him, not much was going on.

He told her that Chukwuma had enemies within and outside the FBI, and none of these enemies is interested in knowing the truth. 'They just want to move on as if nothing happened.' He said. "The committee has met twice but had nothing much to discuss because someone somewhere wants the case closed and buried forever."

But there was one piece of info he gave which Chika found extremely important: The FBI and DNI are planning to break into Room 39 and unravel the secret codes. They want to do that as quickly as possible because that building is very important to National

Security. And the agencies are already on the lookout for qualified people to do that within days.

As he spoke, Chika understood that something fishy was going on; the speed with which things were moving wasn't normal. Not the speed of the investigation, but the speed with which the FBI and the DNI want to gain access into Room 39 is very suspicious.

And her doubts were confirmed when the colleague said to her, ''It appears there's more to just knowing how to get out of that room; it seems like there's something that was kept inside the room that they wish to take back.''

After Chika heard those words, she decided to get in there and exit before them. She enquired of when the Room break was to occur and was told that it would be done in the coming days, three days at most from now. Chika hadn't much time to prepare, but she's worked with short notice all her career and was never going to back down.

The colleague however warned her, "Ma'am, I sincerely think you should leave this case. Allow them to do what they want and later we'll dig more. Act as if you aren't interested in this case until you're restored to the office. Then, we'll do our private investigation and unearth the facts. The atmosphere in the office is tense; there's suspicion everywhere. Please, stand back and let them do their thing. I have a sensation that these people are willing to kill anyone who stands in their way."

Chika nodded in agreement and left without saying a word.

That night, Chika tells her father Dede of her plans to go inside Room 39 and know what the FBI and whoever it was kept inside that place. In her opinion, whatever item it was, held the key to unravelling the mystery surrounding Chukwuma's death, and maybe that of Ikem.

Chika spent all night recalling the conversation she had with Chukwuma a couple of weeks back at dinner. She recalls the indications and codes that were wrapped in weird stories she now wished she had recorded or paid rapt attention to. After a few hours, she was able to recall the secret code for getting into the room and just a portion of the exit code. She knows that the code changes every thirty seconds.

It was going to be a tortuous experience getting in there and getting locked; that could mean her death because she doesn't know who will eventually be walking into that Room and what the person's intentions are. Her desire would be to go in early at 4am and exit the room at 5am with any incriminating item deposited in that Room.

***

Dede couldn't sleep that night. He was lost in thoughts about losing his daughter to the cold hands of death, just as he lost his father (Chika's grandfather). His mind flashed back to his days in the military and how deadly some enemies could be, especially when those enemies include hired assassins on huge pay from drug lords or even governments of nations.

At some point, Dede came down the stairs into the room where Chika was drawing her plans and plotting her strategies. He simply stood at the edge of the door watching her through the small slit Chika had left to monitor the ambient noise. As Dede observes her, he shakes his head and strokes his forehead and hair at intervals.

"I know you're behind me. Don't stay there looking at me; you know you can come in, right?" Chika said, looking at the mirror in front of her, which shows the person at the door. Dede calmly walks in and sits close to the table where Chika is plotting her maps for entrance and exit.

"Don't worry, I'll be fine. I'll be out in an hour or two." Chika said, pausing for a moment as she looked into Dede's eyes.

He strokes his hair and says in a deep hoarse voice, "so, what are your plans?"

"To go in and come out before them," Chika replied.

"I know. But concretely, how do you intend to go in and out seamlessly? Don't you think there are guards 24 hours in and outside the building?" Dede questioned.

"Well, I don't have any business with them. From what Chukwuma showed me, Room 39 should be on the third floor. So, I'll go in through the window of one of the offices on the second or third floor. Find my way to Room 39, get in there, search for whatever item was kept in there and exit the same way I entered."

"And if things go differently? If you're discovered?" Dede questioned further.

"I won't, Dad. I've been there several times and seen the posts where the guards stay. They won't see me at all." Chika replied, trying to dismiss Dede's fears.

"And if things go differently? If this expedition doesn't go like you had thought? Do you have any other plans?" Dede insisted.

"Well, then I'll be constrained to use other means. I hope I don't anyway." Chika answered.

"Fair enough. I would have been shocked if you didn't have an alternative plan… if you weren't going in there with guns, knives and explosives." Dede said.

"Explosives? For what Dad?" Chika said, in surprise.

"For the guards of course. Or for the door to the Room. Or inside the Room. Or for the windows. You never can tell when you'd need what." Dede said, trying to make sense of his advice to carry explosives.

Chika shakes her head, "Dad, it's late. It's 3am and I'll be leaving soon. I plan to get in at 4am and exit at 5am max."

"How about the secret codes for entrance and exit?" Dede asks.

"I have the one for entrance and a bit for the exit, but I'm not so sure. It's complicated." Chika responded.

"I can imagine. That's why I asked that you take explosives with you. Anyway, whatever happens, think of someone or something Chukwuma loves so much if it becomes difficult. Men often use the names of someone or something they love as secret codes."

"Women do that too, Dad." Chika cuts in.

"Yeah, but not like men. Anyway, just remember those he loved while alive. The secret code cannot be far from their names, dates of birth, lovely places they visited, best foods and favourite sports." Dede added.

"Alright, Dad. You're right. I remember that his stories that night, though weird, were centred around places and people he loves so much – his daughter and late wife." Chika responded, carefully omitting that Chukwuma also talked about her so much that night. She thought it wasn't a piece of information worth sharing with Dede. But she kept it in her mind.

Just as Chika was concluding her discussion with her father, she got a call from an unknown line. She felt it could be her colleague in the committee that is calling to give her a vital piece of information at that time. When she answered, the news she heard was saddening.

Unfortunately, her colleague that worked with the committee was killed that night. Chika was shattered by the news; she couldn't help but cry profusely. Her mind ran back to the losses she's experienced recently – the death of Ikem, the murder of Chukwuma and now this.

After a few minutes of crying, Dede advised her to put off her plans towards going into the building tonight, but Chika wouldn't listen. She vehemently refused to back down on her plans. She said that it's better to go tonight than give the enemies another day to strategize and beef up the security in the building. She doesn't know if her colleague confessed to telling her about some vital things before, he was killed. But that's immaterial now. She wasn't backing down, not this time, and not anymore.

So, she took more ammunition than she earlier planned to take. Her initial plans to do things calmly at the building had evaporated with that news; she was ready for whatever or whoever posed a threat to her mission. Her determination was reinvigorated for the sake of those who had died.

It was as if suddenly she entered combat mode; the mode she was in when she travelled to Zumkin to capture Selence. The mode she is in whenever she goes to enemy lands to hunt down terrorists and warlords. The emotion of fear was gone. Courage to do the impossible was found. Mission and only mission was in her mind. Chika was ready to get in there and unearth the truth. For the sake of Ikem. For the sake of Chukwuma. And for the sake of her dead colleague.

CHAPTER 11

D ede had never seen Chika in this mode. She seemed to have a sharpened vision and absolute clarity. She picks up all the materials she needed and tells her father to leave the house with the family until she tells them that she is out of the building and back home. And if she gets trapped inside, they should remain in his house until she gets out. Dede quickly runs upstairs to wake Ebuka and the wife up. He also gets his guns tucked into the holster around his waist, and they exit the house immediately in a bulletproof vehicle belonging to Ikem.

Chika was ready to leave. She slowly bows down to pray, asking God for direction and protection as she goes there. When she was done, she picked up a photo of Ikem and Ebuka, set all the security cameras to record, locked her secure room downstairs and left the house in her bulletproof car. It was now 3.30am and she had 30 minutes to get into that Room and exit in one hour. But even if it takes longer, she was prepared for it this time. Whatever it takes.

Chika arrived at the heavily guarded Antiterrorism Unit building at around 4am. She had driven with her lights off a few kilometres to the building and parked her vehicle a few metres away too. She got out of her car, took all the things she needed and slowly walked towards the building.

From a distance, she had observed that entrance from the main door wouldn't be possible because there were five guards at various corners of the main door. These were the ones she could see. Inside the building, there were certainly several others. So, she opted to enter directly from one of the offices on the first floor. She slowly walks to the back of the building where there were only two guards.

After neutralising them, she climbs the wall and breaks the glass window of the office after carving a circle on it. She was now in. But the main problem is locating Room 39. She quickly takes out her map and torchlight to understand where she was and how to get to Room 39. As she moves to Room 39, she'd meet with five more armed guards who she'd neutralise before finding her way into Room 39.

Chika knew the code to the entrance door because Chukwuma had told her during the dinner they had at his place. She was also aware of how to combine the codes for the exit. Chukwuma hinted at that during his stories but didn't give her a definitive answer on how the combinations go. She just has a list of the countries Chukwuma mentioned and what he did there.

So, she attempted to resolve the puzzle that night before leaving for the building. That way she will be able to go in and out of the building. But when she entered

Room 39 and the door locked, getting the stolen items from CODE RED, and exiting the Room proved way more difficult than she had ever imagined. This begins the phase of escape from Room 39.

***

The three days that the Collingahs gave to Mbe and his cohorts to provide the stolen items have passed, and the drugs were nowhere to be found. Mbe had committed a blunder and his wife, and the families of his colleagues will likely pay for it.

Mbe knew what would happen that night if he didn't get back to the Collingahs. So, he quickly contacted the Collingahs to narrate what happened at the building and promised to get the items as soon as possible. He pleaded with them to spare his wife and colleagues' families.

Chukwuma hadn't revealed the secret code into Room 39 before his death, so the investigators couldn't get into the place to determine if the killer was in there and probably unravel the reason why Chukwuma's body was just at the entrance into the Room. So, the DNI and FBI Directors decided to search for ways to gain access into the Room without destroying the entire building. It was meant to be done very secretly without the knowledge of neither the public nor the employees of the two agencies.

When Mbe and his cohorts learnt of the move, they decided to play an important role in the choice of who gets in there. In their view, if they can know the person or even choose the person, they could make the person get the stolen items for them. So, they all met and decided to visit the University on Pirro's Lane to search for a mathematician or an engineering professor with experience in building or breaking secret codes of banks, safe houses, security agencies – a professional hacker, basically. They didn't want to get a street hacker for fear that the agency wouldn't accept such a person because the security code and other secrets of the agency were at stake. So, a university staff with a verifiable history is preferable.

The next day Mbe and a colleague went to the university to search for Professor Ejike. They've made enquiries on the University archives and asked around to determine who to choose. Ejike stood out from the rest of the people because he's done multiple research projects in the field of security and at one point was called by the government to participate on an inter-ministerial committee for restructuring in the University degree programs. So, he will be doing a very rewarding national service both financially and career-wise.

***

Albert Ejike is a well-esteemed mathematician at Pirro's university. Loved by all, he is a young man who has risen through the ranks in the academic staff through hard work and sound character. With over one hundred publications before age 33, Ejike was made an assistant professor to the admiration of his students and the envy of his fellow researchers. He was nicknamed Albert Einstein, and no one had any doubts that he was on his way for a Nobel prize sometime in his lifetime – the question was just when, not if.

Ejike was in the lecture hall when Mbe arrived at the university in search of him. His office staff asked them to wait until Ejike was done for them to speak with him. Instead of sitting, they preferred looking around the university, deciding to return once Ejike was done.

When his lecture was over, Ejike returned to his office to learn from his secretary that two visitors were waiting to see him from the government. At first, he didn't quite understand the purpose of the visit. When he was called to serve in the committee for university restructuring, he only reserved an email and a call; there was no need for an official visit to his office to communicate the news to him. And there was no prior call or contact before this physical meeting. He didn't know what to expect but was obliged to see them.

Once Ejike got inside his office, he asked his secretary to invite his visitors into his office. Seated behind his semilunar table with a burgundy leather fitting, Ejike welcomed his government visitors to his office with a handshake.

'Good afternoon, sirs.' He said

'Good afternoon, Mr Ejike.' They replied.

Ejike was a bit surprised by the way they called his name as someone they had known for several years.

'Please you may have your seats.' Ejike said, pointing at the two armchairs before his table. 'Would you mind a cup of coffee or water?' he proceeded.

'No, not at all. We're fine.' They chorused.

'Ok, I understand. If at some point you need something, kindly let me know and I'll get that for you.'

'That's ok.'

Ejike couldn't help but notice that Mbe kept looking around since he entered his office. He was looking at the walls, photos, curtains, awards, door, windows, just everything. This he did throughout the entire discussion barely making a 5-second eye contact with Ejike.

This troubled Ejike more because he couldn't tell if he was under some investigation, but he preferred to allow them to act the way that seemed right to them. One thing was fixed on his mind, whatever is the request, the answer would be a capital NO. He had an intuition from the time that they walked into his office that he wouldn't want to work with nor for this type of people, no matter who sent them, including the President.

'Alright, Mr Ejike, we are here on an official assignment by the FBI and DNI. It's a top-secret assignment and no one should ever know that we were ever here. You mustn't tell anyone about our meeting.'

'Alright, Sir.'

'You must have read in the newspapers about what happened in the new Antiterrorism Unit building. We are here because we need your assistance to get into a particular part of that building and to extract some information there. All you must do is get in there and extract the items we will tell you, get out and give them to us and we're done.

For this official job, you'll receive recompense from the government agencies involved and some recognition as well.' Mbe's colleague said, forcing a smile.

All the while they spoke, Ejike simply nodded and pondered little over what they were saying. He had already decided to refuse their offer and was waiting for them to get done with their stories before asking them to leave politely.

'Alright, Sir.' Ejike said smiling. 'I'd love to think about it and get back to you soon. I understand it's delicate and urgent, that's why you came in person to me. But I also have so many engagements this period. So, I'd like to take a few days to see if I can reorganise some of these schedules and then I'll get back to you. I'll then tell you if I'll be able to embark on this project or not.'

'Ok. Hmmm… you won't have a few days because it's quite urgent. We will be expecting your response by tomorrow noon if you wouldn't mind. It's quite urgent and the FBI wants to tidy up this whole investigation and issues around it before the week runs out. So, please tell us by tomorrow morning when you intend to come to do this official assignment. We'll be waiting.' Mbe said, beaming a false smile.

'Tomorrow is too soon for me. I can't give you a call tomorrow.' Ejike said.

'Don't worry, you'll give us a call, or we'll call you if that makes you feel better.' Mbe tapped Ejike's table three times as they stood to leave.

'Who's the lady on the frame behind you?' Mbe questions.

'That shouldn't be any of your business.' Ejike responded.

'I know. It's just that I was wondering what a lady's photo is doing in your office seeing you aren't married, and your parents and siblings don't live in the city.' Mbe added.

'Please, I thought you came on an official assignment. What has my family got to do with the assignment?' Ejike quizzed.

'It's ok. It's just for the sake of curiosity, so we know who our man that is getting into the building is. A sort of background check.' Mbe said, winking at his colleague.

'Alright, I'll be leaving now because I have another lecture to attend. So, you need to leave as well.' Ejike said.

'OK. we'll talk tomorrow then.' Mbe concluded.

After his lecture that day, Ejike went to his laboratory to carry out some experiments. He stayed back at the university until 8pm before going home. Unknown to him, these corrupt FBI agents came back to the university compound later in the day to monitor him. So, when Ejike left, they also followed him closely in their vehicle to know his habitation.

***

The following day, Mbe called Ejike's office. The FBI seem to be close to getting someone to get into Room 39, and Mbe knows that if they get someone before Ejike responds, he will lose everything – the drugs, documents, his wife, and his colleagues. He was not ready to take chances, so he wanted to persuade Ejike to accept his proposal and show up at the FBI office before the weekend.

Worse still was that there were no other options available to him besides Ejike. He got the contacts of some hackers in the country, but none of them boasts the clean background that Ejike has; you can't possibly hand over the most secured room of the antiterrorism unit to a street hacker – he'd convert the data in that place to a personal gold mine.

When Mbe called that morning, the secretary refused to pass the call to Ejike, saying that Ejike was in the lecture hall. Mbe called multiple times afterwards but either received the same response or had his call denied because Ejike had instructed his secretary never to let them back in when they come around nor pass their calls to him. He didn't want to have anything to do with them after the first encounter.

When Mbe saw that Ejike deliberately didn't want to take his calls, he decided to take drastic action that would make Ejike succumb.

***

At 6pm Ejike left the University premises for his house because he has a dinner appointment with someone special to him at 7pm.

When he got home, he quickly freshened up before heading to a restaurant that is located 15 minutes from his house. While following him, the agents observed that he stopped after a few blocks to pick up someone, a young lady, who they could not readily identify but who they suspected was the lady in the picture frame at Ejike's office.

When Ejike stopped and entered the restaurant with the young lady, Mbe and his colleague were able to see her face better. Finally, they have gotten someone through whom they can persuade Ejike to do their bidding.

So, while Ejike and the lady were at the restaurant, Mbe drove back to the building where the young lady was standing when Ejike stopped to pick her up. He began to ask if the people living there knew who she was, feigning to be a friend. With the answers he got, he found out that she is fondly called Ola, a short form of her name Olamma.

Olamma is a very beautiful young lady in her mid-twenties. She graduated in architecture a few years ago and was working with one of the construction companies in the region. A very focused and brilliant lady, she had trained herself through school by working full-time summer jobs and part-time jobs during school sessions. Her father, Ezenna, died from complications of untreated diabetes 10 years ago. And her mother, Ezinne, is a schoolteacher in an elementary school in her village. After her studies, Olamma relocated to the city to work, so she can raise some money to take care of her ageing mother.

A few weeks ago, Ezinne was diagnosed with cervical cancer. She had gone to her gynaecologist for a scheduled visit, and while the gynaecologist performed a pelvic examination, she decided to also perform a pap smear. When the results came back, some abnormalities were discovered. On further examination (CT scan) it was observed that Ezinne had stage II cancer. The doctor recommended that she undergoes a radical hysterectomy and radiation therapy afterwards.

When the doctor called Olamma to break the news to her, she was very devastated to hear it. She is the only child, and her mother is the only one she has alive. Another issue is the money needed for the treatment. Although she told them to go on with the surgery, she wasn't sure of how to raise the money. And she didn't want to disturb Ejike. Although she tried to act strong because of her mother, within her she wished this never happened.

That evening when she went out with Ejike, she had wanted to tell him what was going on but on second thought, decided to do that when she returned from seeing her mother. She informed Ejike that she was travelling the next day to see her mom, and she would be away for a week. When Ejike wanted to know why the sudden need to travel, she just told him that the mom needed emotional support.

***

When Mbe got to Ola's building, he was able to speak with a few people that knew her, who described her as a peace-loving young lady with a good heart. They also told him about the family and how she works so hard to take care of the mother. It was during one of the discussions that Ola's neighbour told Mbe concerning Ezinne's ill health and how Ola needed money for her treatment. Initially, Mbe seemed to be moved with pity and had almost called off their plans to use her as bait to get Ejike. But when he remembered his wife and the other colleagues in the hands of the Collingahs, his mind changed once again. And he decided to exploit Ola's situation.

That evening, the corrupt FBI agents took about three hundred thousand dollars, a fake passport, and a gun, put them into a bag and brought them into Ola's room. While she was at the restaurant with Ejike, they sneaked into her room and carefully dropped the bag where she could see it, beside her bed.

When Ola got back to her apartment that night, she was tired and simply moved to her bed. As she was about to lay down, she observed that there was a bag beside her bed. Curious to know what was inside, she opened it and in shock discovered that it was filled with money. She was confused as to who might have gotten into her room and dropped the money.

She looked around her room, checked her window and door to be sure that no one entered. Then called her neighbour to know if someone came into her room while she was away. Her neighbour said no but pointed out that a man came that evening searching for her. She asked for the name, but her neighbour couldn't tell.

Ola simply moved the bag to a corner in her room. Although the temptation to take part of the money at least for her mother's treatment was much, she refused and decided to take the money to the nearest police station the next day.

***

Unfortunately for her, at 6am, while she got ready to leave the house, a knock was heard at the door. When she answered the door and opened it, she was greeted with an unexpected question from two men she had never met in her entire life.

'Where is the money?' One shouted repeatedly.

'What money, please?' Ola responded, innocently.

'Young lady, where's the money you stole from him?' He shouted more.

'Stole from who? I'm not a thief. I didn't steal any money from anyone.' Ola responded, further confused than in the beginning.

'Inspector, search every corner of this apartment.' Mbe said, signalling one of his corrupt colleagues. 'You'll tell us if you're a thief or not when we have found the money you stole from the man after shooting him dead.' Mbe said, adding an accusation of murder into the mix.

'What?! I shot someone to death! Wait… wait… wait… what's happening here? Do you even have a warrant to search my house? Why would you come into my house this morning accusing me of killing a person and stealing his money?' Ola shouts, disoriented, confused and angry.

'Well, here is the warrant.' Mbe pulls out a fake warrant bearing Ola's name and address.

The other corrupt agent goes in to search her room and sees the bag by the corner of her bed. He also sees Ola's luggage arranged for travel.

'Here is the bag Sir. I also see that she has already packed her luggage for escape this morning. Had we not arrived now, she would have escaped.' He added.

'Wait, I can explain. Please, I can explain.' Ola says while holding back tears. 'I came home last night to see that bag by my bedside. I don't know who dropped it here nor how the person came in. And I intended to take it to the police station this morning on my way to see my sick mother. Please, I didn't kill anyone, and I don't even know the owner of the bag.' Ola explains.

'Young lady, you're lying.' Mbe said.

'Here is the passport and the gun inside the bag too.' His colleague said.

'Don't touch the gun with your hands because her fingerprints are on it.' Mbe responded.

'I didn't kill anyone, please. I only saw the bag when I came in last night. When I saw the content, I decided to take it to the Police this morning. I didn't kill anyone. I don't even own a gun. Last night I went out to the restaurant and afterwards came home. I didn't do any of these.' Ola couldn't hold back her tears anymore. She didn't know what was going on, nor what to even think of what was going on. It was as if the entire world was caving in on her – her mother is seriously sick, she has no money to pay for her treatment and now this litany of accusations for something she knows absolutely nothing about. What on earth has she done to deserve such a cocktail of sad occurrences.

'Young lady, we will be charging you with first-degree murder, possession of illegal firearm and theft. The man you killed is an FBI agent. So, you can be sure that your case is very serious.' Mbe claimed.

'But I did none of these, Sir. Please, you need to hear me out first. Please, Sir, help me. I'm innocent.' Ola pleads, running from Mbe to his colleague and back.

'I have a very sick mother who needs a surgical operation. I'm travelling home this morning to see her before the surgery. Please, can I go and see her? I promise you that I'll return to prove that I did none of the things you're accusing me of. Someone wants to frame me up for something I have no idea about. You can ask my neighbours. I'm a law-abiding citizen, please.' Ola cries.

'No need for that. Olamma. That's your name, right?' Mbe asks.

'Yes Sir.'

'You can sit down.' Olamma sits and Mbe sits by her side.

'Olamma, you want to travel to see your sick mother, right?' Mbe asks.

'Yes, please. I need to see her immediately, else she dies.' Ola responds, with tears flowing down her cheeks.

'Ola, you see, this case is a very serious one – killing a person, stealing his money, and possessing an illegal firearm. These are serious accusations and just be sure that you'll end up in jail for the rest of your life.' Mbe hints, as Olamma continued sobbing while confessing her innocence.

'But we can help you,' Mbe continued. 'You just need to do one thing for us, and we'll act as though this case never existed. We'll take back the bag to the police and tell them that we recovered the bag by the wayside and couldn't find the thief. But if you think you can't do what we want, then we'll arrest you and you won't be able to see your mother for a long time. It's up to you. The decision is yours to make.' Mbe says.

'Whatever you want me to do, I'm willing to do it. I need to see my mother alive, please.' Ola begs.

'We need you to convince Ejike to do what we've asked him to do. Just tell him that if he doesn't do what we've told him, you'll be jailed for life and your mom will die. We're also willing to take care of the medical bill of your mom as a bonus to you.' Mbe concludes.

'Is that all?' Ola asks.

'Yes, that is all. Simple.' Mbe says.

'But what did you ask him to do, please?' Ola asks further.

'Well, that's none of your business. Just convince him to do what we've asked him to do, and you've done your part. Then we'll do ours.' Mbe responds.

'Hmm… ok… ok. I'll talk to him and convince him.' Ola accepts

'If you try to run away or tell anyone what has happened, we will find you and you won't be happy with what will happen. Remember that your fingerprint is on the gun and everywhere on the money and passport. And we saw the items in your room, and you were about to run away with them.' Mbe's colleague adds.

Olamma agrees and gets ready to go meet Ejike as both men leave her room after taking some pictures.

CHAPTER 12

Ejike was expecting Ola's call to tell him when she leaves the city for home. But instead of the call, he heard a knock on his door at about 7am. He was pleasantly surprised to see that the person behind the door was Ola. It's been a while that Ola came around to visit him. Both are principled Christian believers, but Ejike would love her to visit a few times instead of constantly talking at a restaurant or in school or somewhere outdoors.

Ola on her part would also like to but wouldn't want anything that would make them fall short of the vow they took on chastity before marriage. She was sure of herself to a good extent that she wouldn't initiate anything unholy, but you can't control emotions at times, more so the emotions of someone else.

'Good morning, Ola. Please, come in. How're you doing?' Ejike asks as he opens the door.

'Just fine.' Ola barely responds.

Ola strolls into the apartment with heavy eyes and an air of dejection all over her. She had tried to empty her heavy heart in the bathroom before leaving her apartment, but on her way to Ejike's house, the entire weight of her mother's health condition came back to her, and she couldn't hold it.

'Ola, you neither look okay nor sound okay. What's the matter, please?' Ejike asked again.

'It's nothing. Just… nothing. Don't worry, I'll be fine. I just came to tell you that … that I'll be travelling to see my mother.' Olamma said, with her eyes looking down to avoid Ejike noticing that she's been crying for some time.

'Alright dear, but you already told me that last night. And we agreed that you'd call me before leaving.' Ejike says, sensing that there must be something more to this visit than what she's saying.

'And that's what I came to do, to tell you that I'm leaving. Instead of calling, I preferred coming in person.' Ola responds.

'Okay. But why are your eyes heavy? It seems you've been crying all night. What happened to you? Talk to me. Dear, please, can you tell me what's wrong. Maybe I can help. Whatever it is, you know I'll do anything for you.' Ejike insisted.

Ola kept mute, but the tears were gathering. She knew that if she opened her lips to talk, the next thing that would come out would be crying. So, she looked in the opposite direction and tried to distract herself with the piece of paper on the table.

'Ola, please, what's the matter? You look sorrowful, What's the problem? Is your mom, ok? Is everything good at home? Did anyone die? Did you receive bad news from your place of work?' Ejike gently insists, trying to figure out what may have gone wrong between the time they left each other last night and this morning.

While the last set of questions was still on his lips, Ola simply got up and walked to the bathroom, shut the door, and sobbed for a few seconds before letting her tears flow uncontrollably. Ejike didn't know what to do, whether to go into the bathroom to console her or just stand by the door waiting for her to come out. After two minutes of hearing Ola's cries, he opted for the first option. He couldn't stand there hearing her cry without trying to know what the problem was.

'It's ok dear. Please stop crying. It's alright… it's alright. We can sort it out no matter what it is.' Ejike said, trying to console her. He has never seen Ola this vulnerable before him, and he was confused as to what may have broken this beautiful lady.

'Please, can you talk to me… did anyone hurt you? Did someone die? How's your mom? Ola, please, talk to me.' Ejike asked, pausing each time to see if Ola would say anything or even make a gesture to suggest that any of the questions were plausible.

After about three minutes of pouring her heart out in tears, Ejike helped her to wipe her tears and clean her face. Her eyes were visibly red as she stood before the mirror trying to put herself together to explain all the troubles, she's going through to Ejike.

'Can we go to the sitting room or kitchen to talk? I think it'd be better if we sat down. You can take your time, and I can make you something to eat or drink while we discuss. Is that okay?' Ejike appeals.

Ola simply nods and slowly walks towards the door while Ejike follows a step behind, wrapping his right arm around her shoulders.

As they sit down, Ejike quickly gets her a cup of tea, some slices of bread and a bottle of water. Ola gently sits on the sofa opposite the TV set in Ejike's sitting room with her head leaning on her carpus and intermittently rotating along the sulcus of her curved palm.

'You know I told you about the health condition of my mom,' Ola began

'Yes, you did.'

'The truth is that she isn't just ill, but she has cancer... a stage II cervical cancer.' Ola mutters while holding back tears. She bends down to take another handkerchief from her handbag before proceeding with the story.

'Last week, the surgeon called to tell me that she must be operated on and undergo radiation therapy for her to have any chance of survival. I didn't want to disturb you with the whole thing because I know how much you've been through, and how tender your heart could be at times,' she continued.

As she talked, Ejike listened attentively, not knowing what comforting words to speak. Although he hasn't had someone live with or die from cancer, he understands what it feels like to have someone terminally ill; he knows what it feels like to lose someone close to your heart. He lost his elder brother eleven years ago in a car accident.

At the time, he was still doing his PhD program at the university. One afternoon while he was in the laboratory, he received a call that his attention was needed at Chibyke's Medical Centre because his brother, Udoka was involved in a car accident. Udoka was like a father to Ejike.

They had both grown without their father whose death is shrouded in mystery. While official reports say that he died in active service in North Africa, other reports hinted that he had died from a mismatched blood transfusion that elicited severe transfusion reactions. The military medical staff was distracted for a moment and didn't check to be sure that his blood group corresponded with that of the donor blood, so Ejike's father was transfused with the wrong blood type. A few minutes after that, he had severe intravascular haemolysis that the medical personnel in the military camp couldn't treat on time. Multiple organ damage occurred, and he died of shock.

When the news of his death was broken to the family, Ejike's mother was pregnant with him. She survived childbirth but the postpartum depression that followed afterwards was something she couldn't recover from. She slumped into drinking and taking hard drugs to the point that Ejike and Udoka were taken away from her by the social services. Since then, the brothers have grown on their own basically, visiting their old mother as often as they can.

Udoka worked from a young age to make sure they fed and went to school. He even paused his studies so that his younger brother could advance. Until Ejike finished his first degree, Udoka made sure he lacked nothing. Afterwards, Ejike began to work, and Udoka would finally finish his first degree in Business Administration and pursue a master's in International Relations.

He was on his way to host the annual conference of the Centre of Commerce when he collided with an oncoming lorry carrying building materials. He was quickly rushed to the Emergency Unit with a severe brain injury. Despite the surgery, he couldn't make it out of the intensive care unit.

Ejike grieved for months for him. Were it not for God and his passion for his profession, it would have been impossible for him to survive; he could have ended up like his mother. The healing process wasn't complete, however, until he met Olamma, a beautiful, caring godly queen who helped him overcome the loss and now has a positive outlook on life.

***

So, when Olamma talked about her mother's sickness, Ejike could feel the pains in her heart through her voice.

'It's alright dear… it's ok. Wipe your tears. It is well. She will survive. She will be fine. God will take care of all that concerns us. He's been with us since birth, and he'll continue to do that even now.' Ejike said, consoling Olamma the best he could.

'Also, the hospital requested that I deposit several thousand. And I don't have much money on me. I was going home to see if I could plead with them to go on with the surgery and radiotherapy, while I come back to the city to see how to raise the money.' Olamma cries as she bares her heart.

'That's ok. You don't need to do that. I mean, you should go home to see your mom, but the bill won't be an issue. We can afford that. Don't worry, she'll be fine, and we'll be fine too.' Ejike says, assuring Ola of his financial support.

'And there's another bigger problem.' Olamma cuts in as she takes a deep breath.

'What is that? Please, go on Ola.'

'Last night after you dropped me off, I went into my room to see a bag beside my bed. When I opened it, I saw some money. Surprised at who dropped the bag, I called my neighbour who told me that no one entered my room all night except for a man who came around asking after me.' Ola said.

'A man? Did she describe the man to you? Do you know him?' Ejike asks, surprised at how a bag of money found its way into Ola's room.

'Yes, but I don't know who he is. Or rather, I didn't know who he was. So, because I was very tired, and had to wake up early to travel this morning, I decided to sleep and take the bag to the police this morning on my way home.' She paused and shook her head, showing regret for taking that decision.

'This morning around 6am, I heard a knock on the door,' she continued, 'some men came into my room saying that they had gotten a tip that the person that killed an FBI agent was hiding in my apartment. They even showed up with a warrant bearing my name. In less than a minute, one of them identified the bag. Besides the money, there was also a gun and the passport of the victim inside.' Ola narrates, crying.

'What?!' Ejike said in shock and disbelief. 'My dear, this sounds like someone is trying to frame you up. We must report to the police immediately and know how to go on with this.' Ejike suggests.

'The strange thing is that they told me that my fingerprints are on the bag, the gun and passport.' Ola continues. 'And seeing that the bag was found in my room, beside the luggage I'm travelling with, it's suspicious that I was planning to run away with the money this morning.' Ola said, shaking her head.

'How can that be?! This whole story is staged. I'm sure that one of the men that came to meet with you this morning is part of this whole pantomime. So, what did they tell you?' Ejike was looking visibly agitated.

'They asked me to do something for them if I wanted them to drop the charges.' Ola responds.

'And what is that?' Ejike asked further.

'They asked me to persuade you to do what they asked you to do.' Ola said, barely looking at Ejike.

'What they asked me to do?' Ejike said surprised at the offer. He didn't immediately remember having dealings with anyone.

166

'Yes, they said that you must get into that room and get them the items they asked you to get for them. That is the only way they'll drop the charges against me.' Ola said.

Ejike was about to tell Ola that those tricks are no problems at all when she told him that the men vowed never to allow her to see her mother if she doesn't convince him to go on this expedition. Ejike was broken, he had thought about going to the police and giving all the details of Mbe and what he was trying to do. He also wanted to call some government officials he knows to see how Mbe could be arrested for staging this alleged murder and theft. But the life of Ola's Mom is on the line and Ola risks going to jail because no one can tell how the court case would go.

'My dear, please, what did they ask you to do? What items are they looking for and where are they?' Ola asks Ejike, ignorant of the demands Mbe had made a couple of days ago, to Ejike.

Ejike narrates the story of how two men came to his office two days ago under the guise of an official assignment from the government. The men claimed to be officials of the FBI and wanted him to get into a secret room at the new Antiterrorism Unit's building and extract some materials for them. But he declined because of his engagements and because those men didn't sound genuine in their words and attitude.

'There's something fishy about their story and behaviour, so, I just wasn't interested in whatever it was, legal or illegal' Ejike says.

After some moment of discussion, weighing the pros and cons, with Ola, Ejike decided that he would do it for the sake of Ola. He asked Olamma to call the surgeon to proceed with the treatment of her mother. Ejike will sort out the hospital bill.

Olamma also had to cancel her trip home because she was afraid that Mbe and his cohorts could trail her down to her hometown; she doesn't want to put her mother's life at risk. She also decided to go with Ejike into whatever secret room the men wanted him to go into. She believes that she is safer with him than going back to stay in her apartment all alone.

***

Ejike and Olamma decided to play along with Mbe, but this time, they wanted to document their meetings as proof for whatever may come up tomorrow. Ejike calls his secretary and asks her to call Mbe for a meeting that afternoon at the university playground. He wanted to meet in the open where Mbe and his colleague won't be able to do anything funny.

When Mbe received the call from Ejike's secretary, he was happy that Ola was finally able to bend Ejike. He quickly called the FBI office, informing them that he had found someone capable that would go into Room 39 by tomorrow or next. He wanted to stop any moves by the agency to recruit someone else for this delicate job.

That afternoon, armed with their minute audio-visual recording devices, Ejike and Olamma waited for Mbe at the park. Mbe arrived alone this time. When Mbe enquired why Ejike and Olamma were together, Olamma told him that she was going to do whatever it takes to save her mother; that she wants to take part in the expedition. Mbe tried to dissuade her, but she insisted.

Mbe agrees and he tells them that the official assignment is to get into the Room and get out in a couple of days. Getting into the secret room won't be much of a problem because the FBI has been able to unravel the entrance code. But getting out is the major issue because the late architect, Chukwuma didn't reveal the exit code before his death. The agency needs someone with Ejike's ability to decipher the code.

Then, there was an unofficial assignment too. There are some precious items inside that room which they must find and get for him when coming out. The items include wraps of confiscated drugs and important reserved documents all hidden in a briefcase inside the room. Those items must not be tampered with and should for no reason be handed over to the FBI except to himself Mbe.

Mbe informed them that many lives are at stake because of the items in that briefcase. He has also scheduled a meeting at the FBI office with the Director; they should simply show up at the scheduled time, and with their credentials, they'd easily pass the selection process.

During the entire discussion, Ejike deliberately avoided bringing up what transpired that morning between Ola and Mbe. He just wanted Mbe to give out as many details regarding the expedition as possible.

When Mbe was done, Ejike had only one question, 'did you have to go that far to get my attention?' To which Mbe responded, 'when the lives of the members of your family are on the line, a man does whatever it takes to save them. Do whatever you have to do, and your family members will live.' That was all that Ejike needed, a recorded confirmation that Mbe orchestrated the whole drama that took place in Ola's apartment that morning.

Prior to this time, Ejike had been reading the online publications by Kean, the journalist, which Chukwuma was passing to him via emails. He was just doing that as a way of exercising his intellectual ability to solve puzzles, not because he needed the money that Chukwuma had promised. So far, he thinks that he has solved all the puzzles published by Kean correctly. So, he had a few hypotheses as to what the exit code could be. Chukwuma didn't release all the combinations of the exit code from Room 39 before his murder. Ejike wasn't aware of this, neither was Ola.

***

Chika had been trailing Mbe since the day she observed that Mbe was stalking her. She had employed a female private investigator to monitor him. When Chukwuma was killed, Chika's suspicion towards Mbe increased.

There were a few reasons why Mbe could be responsible, the major one being jealousy.

One day, the private investigator called to tell Chika that Mbe was around the university arena in search of a university lecturer named Ejike. When Chika checked, she discovered that Ejike is a mathematician who has worked with the government a few times on academic issues. She didn't quite connect the dots immediately.

But when she remembered that her colleague in the investigation committee said that the FBI was searching for someone or some people to break into Room 39, she quickly connected the dots; Mbe was searching for his man to get in there. So, she figured out that there must be more to this story; something more that could reveal the reason behind the brutal assassination of Chukwuma.

So, during the meeting of Mbe with Ejike and Olamma, Chika came around the university disguised as a female student. She had some shades and a hoodie on, so Mbe won't know she was the one. She sat down a few metres away from them, and from there she took pictures of the meeting. A few times, she would face her video camera towards them and when Ola looked in her direction, she'd bend the camera, pretending to fix the lens. When she was about to leave, Ola observed her hoodie and boots and took note of them.

***

The following day, the DNI and FBI directors invited five people, including Ejike and Ola to the FBI headquarters for a discussion on their assignment before sending them there. The DNI Director wanted to tell them how important and confidential their assignment is, including the risks involved.

During the discussion, he explained to them that there's a high risk that they'd never get out of the Room...alive. He told them that Room 39 is an apartment that is built like a labyrinth. It was intended to be a place that no hacker can infiltrate and no weapon, no matter how sophisticated can penetrate, except for an atomic bomb.

If they got trapped in there, the only other alternative would be to simulate an earthquake of high magnitude, destroy all the security protocols and destroy the Room. It's a security system that the FBI and DNI paid heavily for, and they don't intend to destroy it. This is beside the fact that destroying Room 39 would mean the death of any person inside. Therefore, all of them that are going in there must reflect on these risks and know that it is a mission that has no options, they either exit the Room alive in three days or exit the Room.

At the end of the discussion, two people decided to quit because the compensation was not worth it. Ejike and Ola looked at each other the entire time the Director were explaining the risks involved. But each time they wanted to give up the expedition, they remembered what the alternative was – constant fear for their lives and those of their family members. So, they decided to stay put, if they perish in the rubbles of the earthquake, so be it.

The other person that stayed put was Kachi. Yes, the middle-aged professor of Chemical engineering who synthesised the drugs that the Collingahs stole from his laboratory. All the while he seemed so calm about the expedition, asking questions as one who is very determined to get in there and who is partially sure of leaving the Room alive. While the others trembled for their lives, he was busy asking questions about the type of materials used in constructing the building, the doors of Room 39, the planimetry of the apartment and several other questions that were useful but which no one was asking.

The Directors were impressed about his attitude; their hope of finally unlocking the secret code seems founded and it was founded solely on Mr Kachi, a world-renowned chemistry professor. Although his discipline seemed far away from codes and numbers and security, you never can tell what chemical formulas could do, especially in the hands of an intellectual like Mr Kachi.

The only time everyone, including the directors, cringed, was when he asked questions regarding CODE RED, a safe box inside Room 39 that is meant to be top-secret and unbreakable. But he quickly retraced his steps and told everyone that he wasn't interested in it. He just wanted, out of curiosity, to know if they kept something there, they'd want him to get out for them in case there was an earthquake; at least that item would be saved even if all of them died. Everyone laughs but he knows where he is going.

While everyone's objective was to decipher the exit code, Kachi had a two-fold objective or rather three, but two inside the Room – firstly, to lay his hands on the drugs he synthesised, secondly, unravel the code and thirdly, to make the Collingahs pay for what they did to him.

***

Kachi's interest in the puzzle since learning from the newspaper that the Collingahs were in search of their drugs has increased. Daily, on his way to school, he'd purchase the local newspaper where the puzzles were published and go ahead to solve them. He was convinced that the new Antiterrorism building was in some way linked to the drug that the Collingahs were searching for.

CHAPTER 13

Several weeks have passed since Kachi began to solve the puzzles. On many occasions, he has thought of contacting the journalist to learn more about who was passing those puzzles to him and maybe get to meet with whoever it is in person. Maybe the person has a way to get into the building where the drug is kept, and he'll be able to recover his drugs.

But after some moments of consideration, Kachi would defer. He felt it wasn't time yet to meet with a journalist who may likely disclose his hiding location and make the Collingahs come after him again. He wanted to remain in the dark, at least for now.

However, when the news of Chukwuma's death broke, Kachi felt it was time to act, especially seeing that he was killed in the building premises. He had no idea whether Chukwuma died inside or outside the building, but he knew that Chukwuma's death would raise so much dust that before it settled many things could have happened underneath. The death of Chukwuma in his opinion wasn't planned, so, whoever committed that murder would be searching for a way to cover it up.

***

One evening, Kachi decided to write to Kean, the journalist, anonymously. He told the journalist that he had some interesting news regarding the death of Chukwuma, and if he wanted to know more, he should contact him within 24 hours, or he'll miss the chance of having an exclusive big story for his online audience.

When the journalist read the mail, he was convinced that it was a big story that he couldn't afford to miss. So, he responded the next morning informing Kachi that he was ready to meet with him. When Kachi read the response of Kean, he was excited. Although he didn't have any interesting news to share regarding the death of Chukwuma, he decided to go anyway. At worst, he'd cook up something to share with Kean.

Kachi wrote back to him, asking that they meet at 9pm in one of the restaurants outside the city, to which the journalist obliged.

That evening before heading for the meeting, Kean hid some recording devices in both his jacket and rucksack. Kachi on his part has learnt to be very careful and a little investigative in attitude after his experience with the Collingahs. So, he also brought an mp3 recorder with him to the meeting. Before they exchanged pleasantries, Kachi turned on his recording device. He has learned the hard way not to trust anyone. They both ordered a plate of risotto ai funghi and a bottle of red wine.

The owner of the restaurant is an Italian immigrant named Chirico, a friend of Kachi. Kachi and Chirico became friends after he moved to live in the peripheries of Pirro's Lane. Not having a wife nor children to help him cook, or access to the luxurious restaurants in the city centre, Kachi resorted to eating by this local restaurant. That doesn't mean that Chirico's restaurant isn't good, far from it, but compared to the luxurious atmosphere of the restaurants located on Pirro's lane, we can say that Chirico is a local champion with a menu that matches the best Italian restaurants in the city.

As they sat down waiting for their risotto ai funghi to be served, the journalist thought it was time to break the ice.

'So, you had something to tell me regarding the death of Chukwuma,' he said.

'Shshsh… calm down young man,' Kachi whispers, signalling Kean with his hands to relax and wait for his meal. 'I know that you want to know the interesting story, and I'm going to tell that to you. But we must enjoy our meals first. Risotto ai Funghi is an important meal for Italians, and I don't think the owner of this restaurant would be happy hearing us share spy stories here and now.' Kachi smiles.

'But no one can hear us.' the journalist insists.

'You never can tell. You can't be too sure, my dear. These inanimate walls have ears and sometimes can gossip more than we humans.' Kachi giggles.

'Oh, there it is… my risotto ai Funghi, hmm… italicious,' Kachi continues as he inhales the aroma emanating from the contents on the brown ceramic plate.

'Please, the glass of wine. Because you know that they go together, else you won't enjoy this Italian delicacy.' he says to the waiter.

They both grab their cutleries and begin to empty the plates into their breadbasket.

'So, for how long have you been doing this?' Kachi breaks the peaceful silence.

'Doing what?' asked Kean.

'Working as a journalist.' Kachi responded.

'For a long time.' Kean responded.

'And that means?' Kachi asks further.

'For over 6 years.' The journalist replied.

'Ok. You are well vast to be in this business for just 6 years. It shows that you read a lot. I read most of your write-ups and they're full of interesting pieces of knowledge. I love that you do your research before publishing anything.' Kachi said, showing his admiration for the intellectual and writing skills of the young journalist.

'Thank you, Sir. That's normal for us journalists.' Kean said.

'No, not so. I have seen very bad journalism recently. People that don't know anything and do not make efforts to verify their stories are writing the front pages of newspapers and having viral contents.' Kachi insists, returning to his earlier point.

'Well, there are always those types of people in every sector Sir.' Kean points out.

'That's true, but journalists should be very careful. Words have power, especially when they come from someone people trust should know his or her stuff.' Kachi said.

'You're right. But you haven't told me who you are and what you do.' the journalist cuts in.

'Well, I'm a chemical engineering professor at the university close to us here. I'm also a researcher with one of the most important laboratories in the nation. Or rather, I had one of the most important laboratories in the nation with a great team of biologists, bioengineers, oncologists, paediatricians and gynaecologists working for an important cause.' Kachi said with a sad tone.

'So, what happened, why did you say, 'you had?' Did it burn down? You lost the funding you had or you're now on pension? You don't look that old to me, but who knows.' The journalist asked.

'Well, that's why I called you. To tell you what happened.' Kachi responded.

'Okay, that sounds interesting. I mean, I'd like to have the answers to all the questions I just asked, but when you say that you called me just for that, then it doesn't sound so good. That wasn't the agreement we had. You invited me for an exclusive story on the death of Chukwuma.' Kean says, showing some disappointment.

'And that's what I'm about to tell you; the exclusive story I told you about.' Kachi responds.

'Wait, are you saying that you killed him, or you know someone that killed him?' Kean asks.

'Oh, come on! This is the reason I said that you journalists need to verify things. You're already rushing so fast to a conclusion without relaxing to let me speak.'

Kachi says, showing his displeasure at what Kean had just said.

'I'm relaxed, but I also need to ask questions. That's what a journalist does too.' Kean insists.

'Alright, if you want to ask questions all night without listening, then, we call off the meeting. I'm sorry for inviting you. Don't worry about the bill, I'll take care of it. You can take your leave now.' Kachi says, rising from his chair.

'Chirico... Chirico my friend, I'm done. I'll be going now because this young lad doesn't understand what's going on. He thinks Pirro's Lane is all gold and glamour, beautiful ladies and nice cars with great architecturally designed buildings,' Kachi continued.

'He thinks he understands it all because he secretly receives puzzles that he publishes weekly. His source is dead, and his career is about to tank but he doesn't know it.' Kachi concluded, as he moved the chair backwards and headed towards the cashier.

When the journalist heard that, he realised that Kachi isn't a timewaster after all; if Kachi knows that it was Chukwuma that sent the puzzles to him, then he certainly knows so much more.

'Oh, I'm sorry Sir. I'm so sorry. It hasn't gotten to that. I'm sorry for the way I acted. It's just that I came with a mind to hear what you had to say concerning the death of Chukwuma.' Kean begs.

'And I told you that I'm going to tell you that. It's part of my story. Just be patient.' Kachi responds.

'Ok Sir, I'm sorry. I'm so sorry. Can we sit back down and continue our discussion, please?' Kean asks.

'It's ok.' Kachi adjusts himself and sits back. 'Please, let's have coffee.' Kachi says, turning to the waiter.

'Can I record the discussion, Sir?' Kean asks.

'Sure, you can. I'm recording too. I've learnt not to trust anyone.' Kachi answered.

'Alright. You didn't ask for my permission to record our conversation, but it's alright.' Kean said, a bit shocked that Kachi has been recording the conversation.

'I'm sorry for the way I spoke a few seconds ago. Truly, I called to tell you what I know concerning the death of Chukwuma, but I also want something from you,' Kachi says. 'What you'll get from me will help you understand the circumstances surrounding his death, but what I want from you will help to unravel the person that killed that great architect. It's something we should do together, for the sake of this man.' Kachi posited.

'Okay. So, what do you want from me and what do you want to give to me?' The journalist asks.

'Let's start with what I'll give to you: this is a story that began several months ago, which no media house covered because it was actually done in secrecy so that nothing gets out. This is the story of a pill that was meant to serve cancer patients, but evil minds intended to use it for a different purpose. That is the origin of this whole drama that is unfolding today.'

Kachi goes on to tell him the whole story of the drug he synthesised in his laboratory and how the Collingahs destroyed his laboratory and carted away all the documents and drugs. Then, how some corrupt FBI agents stole those drugs and probably hid them inside that building. He then suggested that Chukwuma may have been killed because of those stolen items.

'I don't know if he was killed by the corrupt FBI agents or the Collingahs, but I'm sure that if we could get into that building and find those stolen items, we'll hold the key to unravelling who the murderer is.' Kachi said. 'This way, Chukwuma will truly have justice and I will also have justice for the wrong that the Collingahs did to me and my staff.' Kachi concludes.

When he was done with the entire story, the journalist knew what Kachi wanted, and he was willing to give it to him without questions. Kachi needed the rest of the puzzles that Chukwuma had sent to the journalist. He wants them so he can decipher the exit code of Room 39.

While Kachi was bent on laying his hands on those drugs and then punishing the Collingahs, the journalist was interested in making Mbe, the Collingahs and whosoever partook in the killing of Chukwuma pay. The exclusive story, which Kean could turn into a series on his website, is just a pleasant addition.

The main issue now is how to get Kachi into the Antiterrorism building, but most importantly into Room 39. At this moment, they have no idea how that would happen, but they are sure an opportunity would soon present itself. They just need to be prepared for it and patiently wait.

The journalist promises to send Kachi the most recent puzzles that Chukwuma sent to him over the last week. He was about to publish them on his website before he learnt of Chukwuma's death, so he withheld them. He felt that some ill-intentioned people may be after those codes. These puzzles, according to him, hold the key to discovering who killed Chukwuma.

As the journalist drove home that night, he couldn't stop thinking of the entire story. He has spent over 5 hours with Kachi discussing the entire happenings and was shocked at how many things were going on Pirro's Lane that the entire region wasn't aware of. When this story is over, he promised himself to focus more on investigative journalism; that is where the facts are, not the statements released by politicians or public officials. You need to dig deep to uncover the things that eyes do not see and ears never get to hear.

***

Kean got home at 3am, bodily tired but wasn't feeling sleepy at all. His mind kept running on the best strategy to employ in getting Kachi into that building so he can recover those stolen items.

As he was about to turn on his computer to send the rest of the puzzles to Kachi, he received an anonymous call that warned him to delete all the emails he received from Chukwuma from his email account. He was confused not knowing who it was nor how the person got his phone contact. But after the discussion he had with Kachi tonight, he knew that many things are yet to unfold, and he was ready for them.

He quickly called Kachi to inform him about what just happened. They both agree that he should immediately upload all his important files to the Cloud and encrypt them. He should also copy them to a hard drive and hide it away. Then, he'll grant Kachi access to the files. This way, they won't lose important documents. Afterwards, he should eliminate all the suspicious data from his system.

***

The journalist spent all night working on this and by 8am he was done. Then, just as he was about to call Kachi to grant him access to the files on Cloud, he heard a knock on his door. When he answered the door, he saw three well-built men dressed in black suits standing in front of his door. Without exchanging greetings, they simply told him that they have an order to bring him to the FBI headquarters immediately. When he sought to know the reason for the call, he was simply told that all his questions would be answered at the headquarters. He asks for a minute and quickly gets into the bathroom to urinate.

While he was in the bathroom, he heard some noise in the apartment. When he got out, he saw that the officers were going through his computer systems without his permission. He got angry and shouted at them to stop that immediately, but his shouting fell on deaf ears as they continued unperturbed.

Once he was dressed, they whisked him away to the headquarters. His only prayer was to be alive to tell Kachi what happened to him. While in the bathroom, he had sent an encrypted message to Kachi, telling him the password to the files he uploaded online and informing him that some unknown men were in his apartment to take him to the FBI headquarters.

Unknown to Kachi and Kean, the FBI was searching for people to send into Room 39 to unravel the exit code. When they got to the FBI headquarters, the journalist was ushered into a waiting room. While he was there, he continued sending cryptic messages to Kachi on his whereabouts. Soon the FBI Director appeared and asked him to come over to the meeting hall. In the meeting hall were also Mbe and some other agents. This wasn't his first time seeing Mbe, but he couldn't tell who he was exactly. He had seen him a few times on Pirro's Lane and Quib's Avenue and maybe around the new building, but he couldn't readily tell.

The FBI Director was very scarce with his words. He simply asked if he was receiving some puzzles from the late architect Chukwuma. At first, he wanted to deny but knew that if the FBI invited him in the first place, they must have done their background checks. And since he published them online, it was very possible that someone in the room has read his website and seen it, or someone must have heard about it from somewhere. So, he responded in the affirmative.

The next question was more subtle. The Director wanted to know if any of his readers had sent back answers to the puzzles so far. To this he intelligently declined to answer, citing privacy reasons. On further pressing, he simply told them that people can attempt resolving the puzzles and commenting on his blog posts, but he hasn't checked because the prize will go to the person who solves all the puzzles. That is the agreement. So, he's waiting until all the puzzles have been published before he'd check to see who solved all of them.

The Director now asked him if he was aware that Chukwuma, the man who constantly sent him the puzzles, was late. He said yes that he read about it in the newspapers. They went on to ask him if there were other puzzles Chukwuma sent to him which he is yet to publish. He said that he publishes anyone he receives as soon as he receives them. So, if there were any left, he wasn't aware of them.

Then, the Director asks him if he knew anyone who could solve all the puzzles and get them the correct code that Chukwuma was trying to communicate through the puzzles. Or if the person is willing, he can go with them into the Room to test if the code works. The journalist simply answered that he will send an email to his readers and see who shows up with the correct answers. He had wanted to say yes and mention the name of Kachi, but that would contradict his answer to the second question. The meeting ends with the director informing him that he'd need an answer within 24 hours.

When the journalist got home that day, he used a public phone line to contact Kachi, telling him everything that happened. After much deliberation, they decided to give it a shot. Kachi will be recommended by the journalist to partake in the expedition. He will go in with them to test if the exit code he had gotten from the puzzle worked. But before leaving for the FBI headquarters, Kachi and the journalist spent the day solving the other puzzles that Chukwuma sent, which the journalist hadn't published.

Later that evening, the journalist called the Director's office to inform him that he had found someone who could be of help in resolving the problem of the exit code. He is a well-known professor of chemical engineering from the university and has offered to help his nation in this important mission. This is how

Kachi found himself in this morning's meeting with the FBI and DNI directors.

However, what Kachi and the journalist didn't know is that the exit code isn't complete; there's a tiny but important detail that Chukwuma added that day before he was killed. A detail that only Chika can guess; a detail that seems quite easy, but will her mind ever get there, or will they be trapped in Room 39?

***

The first time that Chika got into Room 39, she was petrified by what she saw. All her imaginations before now can best be described as rudimentary. She had at best imagined the apartment to be simply cosy with a table and chair, a safe box (CODE RED), some shelves for books. She was completely wrong.

The moment the door closed behind her, the entire place turned blue. The light in the room is designed to respond to the feelings of the person in the room. Do you remember when Chukwuma told Chika that the Room is a place they can go in to do several things together? Unless disabled the lights keep changing with changing emotions of the occupant(s).

Room 39 had been constructed with the most sophisticated security fittings available in the country. It is equipped with sensors at every centimetre. When Chika got in, an alert was immediately sent to the Police, FBI and DNI signalling that someone was in the Room. They quickly called the guards in the building but were informed that everything was okay from their end. Chika had changed the settings of all the security cameras leading to the Room, so everything seemed ok.

Another important detail that no one, except Chika and Chukwuma, knew is that Room 39 can be accessed from two places, the first and third floors. The access everyone knew was through the first floor. Chika, being aware of this detail entered Room 39 via the third floor where there aren't any guards deployed. Chika knew this detail because the third floor was meant to house the director's office and those of the top officials of the Antiterrorism agency. It was during one of her routine visits to Chukwuma that he showed her this beautifully designed office and the secret on and in the wall.

Behind Chika's desk is a padded wall, decorated with the most beautiful clothing designs from Africa. If a man of 175cm stood close to the wall behind Chika's desk, equidistant from the two walls on both sides, and rubbed his hand on the wall, he'd notice a little protuberance just at a 45° angle to his right.

That protuberance is a tiny button that is fingerprint sensitive. That is the only point on the entire wall that has a black covering made of Opanteclaus, a refined leaf of a rare plant found in Awo-Omamma, in the Eastern part of Nigeria. It possesses an intrinsic ability to sense human touch and in a second become transparent so that the fingerprint can be read by the sensor attached to it. How Chukwuma laid his hands on Opanteclaus is a story that I'd save for next time. He always leaves his signature in any building he constructs, and this is certainly one of those. Looking at it from a distance, you wouldn't notice any difference from the rest of the patterns covering the wall.

Once the button is activated by Chika's fingerprint, the wall slides both ways and a silent mini elevator appears that takes you to the first floor. On the first floor, there's a different door that leads into Room 39. The door has the same entrance and exit requirements as the main entrance that everyone is familiar with. Chika got in through this door.

CHAPTER 14

S o, when Chika arrived at Room 39, her aim was to search for whatever evidence that shows who killed Chukwuma and why. Then, she'd exit immediately. But that was never going to happen, no, at least not as fast as she had imagined. There were several hurdles to cross, and they won't be as easy as she had imagined.

The first thing to take care of is the presence of anyone inside that Room. The second hurdle would be to find the evidence that shows who killed Chukwuma and why. The third would be to exit the room before Ola, Ejike and Kachi come in. And the fourth would be the security guards in and around the building. It'll be daytime when she leaves the Room, so it's a lot more complicated to handle. But first things first, reconnoitre.

Chika still feared that the killer of Chukwuma was still inside the room since the killer hasn't been found. Maybe he's trapped inside searching for a way of escape, or he could be inside for the same reason Chika came in - the evidence. Chika was unable to hear what Mbe, Ejike and Ola discussed at the university playground, so she couldn't tell if one of them was the killer or they were planning on how to get the killer out of Room 39.

She must, first, get acquainted with the new unpredictable environment. She has observed that the colour as she entered was blue, but once she drew her gun it turned red, so she figured out in some way that the Room's lightning changes are based on movements or actions or something else, but it never remains the same except you're calm. She thought about turning off that setting but decided not to focus on that now until she's sure someone else isn't lurking by the corner to kill her.

She slowly moves around all the rooms not minding the colours that were going bizarre at each turn. Going from one Room to the other, she observes that it felt warmer than her office upstairs, and the source of the heat isn't from the data storage centre located in one of the cubicles in Room 39. When she got into the Data Centre, the place was very cool. Presumably, because of the work that those devices in that cubicle would be doing, an internal and external cooling system was installed to maintain a certain temperature for optimal performance of the devices.

What convinced her the most about the presence of a living organism in Room 39 was when she touched one of the sofas in the sitting room and perceived that the temperature differed from that of the sofa a few metres away; it was warm. That was when her blood cortisol level rose; her fears that the killer could be inside the Room was founded after all, and she did well to come in with her armoury.

As the next door slid open, Chika was met with a projectile aimed at her forehead. Someone had aimed a round object at her that arrived at such a speed that she couldn't dodge the bullet. In the process of falling from the impact of the apple fruit that hit her, a bullet mistakenly left the barrel of her pistol.

Yes, fortunately, it was an apple fruit that met the forehead of Chika although the impact was much given the short-range.

Chika quickly stood to her feet and hid behind the wall in the adjacent room. When she looked around and saw the object that hit her, she was shocked. 'How would someone who assassinated Chukwuma be fighting with an apple fruit? Or is it that the assassin has exhausted his bullets and so resorted to a more rudimentary arsenal?' Chika thought to herself. Anyway, she resolved to be more careful this time. After all, David killed Goliath with a sling and a stone.

As she rose to enter the same room again, another object got fired at her, this time it was a glass cup, which missed its target because Chika was ready this time. As she dodged the glass cup, she was able to see the source of these bizarre weapons and fired a shot in that direction. Her shot missed its target as well. And just before she could fire a second, she heard someone scream, 'Please stop, please I'm sorry, I'm sorry, I'm so sorry; I'm sorry, I'm innocent. I'm just a young lady, please I'm sorry.'

As Chika drew near to see who it was, she was shocked. Never in her wildest imagination could she have thought that the person in front of her would be found in that room ...ever. There was no way she could be there for whatever reason in the entire universe. But there she was, staring at her, in tears, gripped by fear of what her fate will be.

For five seconds Chika didn't know how to initiate the conversation, she was completely lost. The only thing that could come out of her mouth was, 'what are you doing here, Jane?' And obviously, Jane couldn't answer because she was still in tears. 'How did you get in here? Is there anyone with you? Anyone holding you captive?' Chika quizzed further.

'No, there's no one with me. I was afraid when I heard the noise of someone in the apartment and I felt it was the man that killed my father. So, I ran into the kitchen to hide.' Jane says, her voice quavering from days of crying.

'It's okay dear. It's alright. There's no one else, just the two of us… just the two of us. It's alright dear.' Chika embraces Jane, trying to console her. Jane continues to sob as Chika wipes her eyes while looking around the corners of the Room to be sure that no one else was in there with Jane prior to her arrival.

'You said that there's no one here with you, right? ' Chika asked

'Yeah, there's no one. I've been alone for several days here. Maybe up to one week. I can't even tell anymore.' Jane responds.

'One week?! How did you get in here in the first place and why haven't you left?' Chika asked further.

'I got in here the night my father was killed.' Jane said.

'Really? I've been calling you since that night until last night, but your phone wasn't going through.' Chika says.

'Yeah. I turned my phone off because I felt that the people that killed my dad would locate me. I'm afraid they'd come after me to kill me just like they killed my dad.' Jane replies.

'It's alright now. No one will find us. It's OK dear. I'll protect you.' Chika cuddles her, assuring her protection from whoever committed such gruesome murder against her dad.

'Have you eaten something or were the apples your meal?' Chika asks, smiling.

'Yeah, I have eaten although there are not many options in this place.' Jane says.

'I see. Alright dear, I brought something that you can eat so you'll gain some strength. Afterwards, we'll leave this place.' Chika draws her bag and pulls out a big hamburger with cheese and hands it over to Jane.

'But this is junk?' Jane said.

'Well, you don't carry jollof rice and fried turkey when you're preparing for war. If you have time to cook that and package it, then you aren't ready for battle.' Chika interrupted.

'Now, munch on this while I check around this apartment. I had thought that this was a room, but this is just an apartment and a large one at that.' Chika hands over the burger to Jane as she stands up to make sure there was no one in the apartment.

***

When Chika mistakenly fired the shot at Jane, a second alert from Room 39 was sent to the various security agencies. Although the guard monitoring the cameras responded that everything was ok, Mbe wasn't convinced. He had asked one of his men to monitor every movement within and outside the building. So, when the second alert came, Mbe knew that someone was inside the room although he couldn't tell who. Together with his colleagues, they decided to check if Chika was in or outside the building. They knew that she had been suspended from the DNI, but her constant questioning and nosing around could threaten their plans.

Mbe sent two members of his team to Chika's house to verify if she was at home. It was now around 6am, but the people that were sent couldn't find Chika's cars. And after waiting for 30 minutes without observing any movements around the house, they decided to knock on the door. When there was no response, they broke in to discover that no one was at home. Everything seemed normal in the house, apart from the absence of a living soul. There was an exception, a written note on the dining table. On the paper was written, *'I know you'll come after me too, after you killed my colleague. But you know what? I'm ready for you whenever you decide to play seriously. Yours truly, Chika.'*

The CCTV cameras that Chika and Dede had installed recorded them as they exited the house to tell Mbe what they observed. Chika didn't know precisely who killed her colleague cum source, although she placed Mbe at the topmost of her list of suspects. When Mbe learnt of Chika's note, he knew that Chika was convinced that he was responsible for the death of her colleague. So, he decided to play seriously just as Chika had desired.

The truth however is that Mbe wasn't responsible for the death of Chika's colleague, someone else was. Someone who isn't responsible for the death of Chukwuma, but who is happy with his death anyway. But who cares? Mbe already had much blood on his hands, and He wouldn't have any opportunity to explain that to Chika if they ever met. After this, Mbe was fully convinced that Chika had gotten into Room 39 or at least is in that building to unravel who killed Chukwuma.

The next thing to do is to bite Chika where it'd pain her most. So, Mbe decided to find where Chika was hiding Ebuka, her son, since he wasn't in the house. He asked some of his team members to be stationed outside the new building while monitoring the device they had attached to Chika's jacket. The other team will go in search of Ebuka and Dede.

ROOM 39

As Chika searched all the rooms in Room 39, she saw that the place was a well-furnished apartment. Aside from the sitting room, it had kitchens, dining halls, bathrooms, a sauna, a meeting hall, and a very wide room called the Data Centre. All these disguised the fact that the topmost security secrets of the nation are stored here. If you walked into the room from the main entrance, you'd think that it's a presidential suite and nothing more. The security details could as well be found in the best hotels around the world, but if you looked closely, you'd observe that there is so much more than meets the eyes.

As Chika walked around the apartment, her aim was also to find out where CODE RED is and see what the killer may have been looking for. As she searched and searched without finding anything suspicious, she came back and asked Jane if there was anything suspicious that she saw in the Room when she came in. Jane said no that everything inside seemed normal. Chika was rather confused and disappointed that her hypothesis wasn't finding any substrate to work with. Jane noticed this but kept calm.

After some minutes, Chika came back and saw that Jane was done eating. She looked restless and in deep thoughts. Jane on the other hand wondered why she was preoccupied.

'Can we leave now?' Jane asks.

'No! I mean, we can leave but not yet.' Chika answered. 'There must be something here… No, there must be something. It's not possible. There's certainly something in here.' Chika muttered as she thought of areas of the Room she hadn't quite explored properly.

The more Chika talked to herself; the more Jane grew suspicious of her.

'What does she want? The drugs and documents or something else? Could she be an accomplice to the man who killed my dad? Why is she not in a haste to leave? How did she get in here and what's her mission? The night she had dinner with my dad, I noticed that she was unusually calm. What happened when my dad asked me and Ebuka to leave them to discuss?' Jane thought to herself.

As these questions flooded Jane's mind, her assurance of safety in the hands of Chika soon turned into fear for what Chika may do to her. It was as these thoughts ran through her mind that she decided to keep the things she knew about the Room secret.

After some moments of talking to herself, Chika decided to know how and why Jane was in Room 39. It's not a place one would expect to find her, moreover, this should be the most secure place in the country - the famous Room 39 in the Antiterrorism Unit's building. Jane decided to narrate what happened and how she came into Room 39, but she purposely omitted some details regarding CODE RED because she sensed that was what Chika was after.

And she was right. Although Chika wants to save Jane and unravel the reason and person behind Chukwuma's death, she was mostly interested in seeing how that vital information could help her unravel what was most important to her - the death or whereabouts of her dearly beloved husband Ikem. Her unofficial interactions with Chukwuma were all geared towards getting leads. So, even though getting Jane out of that room alive was important to her, the most important thing was finding any evidence that could help with resolving the case of Ike's death. Jane decided to tell her the story of his father's murder anyway, but carefully omitting some vital pieces of information.

***

Jane had come to the office to get her dad some food she prepared for him. Chukwuma was in his office having a meeting with some foreign visitors that wanted his opinion on a maximum-security prison they wanted to erect for people convicted of heinous crimes. The appointment was at 5 pm and Chukwuma knew that he wouldn't be done until 7pm. So, he asked Jane to instead come over to the office so they can have dinner together at 6pm and Jane can go home while he finishes up.

Jane arrived at 6pm and waited for her father to take a break so they could have dinner together. But Chukwuma was so engrossed with the meeting that he asked Jane to wait for a little while. Jane was flying back to school that night. Her short holiday is over and she's due to resume classes next week. Her flight is at 9pm, so she had wanted to spend some time with her dad because she doesn't know when they'd be done.

'Hi darling, I'm so sorry.' Chukwuma pleaded as he exited the meeting room to meet Jane.

'But you can take a break. You can ask them for a 20-minute break so we can eat.' Jane responded.

'Darling, it's just something really important that I need to finish up immediately and let them leave. Please, give me 30 more minutes and I'll be all done. Alright?' Chukwuma pleaded.

'Alright. But remember that I have a flight to catch at 9pm.' Jane says.

'I do my love. I do.' Chukwuma nods as he heads back into the office to tidy up what he was doing with his visitors.

The meeting ended at 7.23pm and Chukwuma was so sorry to have kept her daughter waiting for over an hour now. He decided to appease her in some way but there wasn't anything he could think of. He can't take her out to her favourite restaurant, Chibyke's Delicacies, because it was already late. He can't also take her to Heart Mender's Luxuries, the most exquisite resort on Pirro's lane.

When he couldn't come up with anything, he decided to show her the most sophisticated security fitted room or rather apartment he has ever built. That was a great risk he was taking because he isn't meant to show anyone what is inside there, but since there was nothing else, he could do to pull a smile from this young lady that is leaving for her final year in medical school, his only daughter and mother, he decided to take the risk.

Jane was excited about the idea of seeing this special Room. Chukwuma told her that the entrance code is simple for anyone who speaks the language or who knows the code. But this is simply because the building hasn't officially opened. On the opening day, the DNI and FBI would add the fingerprints of the directors and Chika to it making it more complicated. Also, there's an option of activating the sensor meant for reading the iris. So, it becomes impossible to enter if you aren't in the system. But all these multiple levels of verification aren't active yet, so you can go in with simply IRI ATO NA ITOOLU.

'Coming out, however, is more complicated both now and worse after its activation. Besides the fingerprints and iris sensors that will be activated at the exit too, the code for getting out of the room is a bit bizarre,' according to Chukwuma. 'It's a combination of places I've visited that left a mark in my heart and the fantastic people I met there, including what I did there. And this one has a special kick that I added today, the birthday of a special person that is somehow dear to my heart.' Chukwuma hinted. When Jane enquired to know who it was, Chukwuma declined to tell her, promising to respond once they were on their way home.

***

In Room 39, as Chukwuma nicknamed this special apartment, there are nine doors that can only be seen and opened when you touch the Opanteclaus of each. Jane didn't bother to know the meaning of that word nor its origin. She's used to hearing her father give weird names to things, so she didn't even bother to ask because that would trigger a whole new story, she wasn't ready for.

'Some people think that the only door is this main entrance on the first floor, but there are eight others that are right inside here.' Chukwuma added.

'Now, once you touch the Opanteclaus, a little screen appears for you to input the code. The nine all use the same code, but there is a further security check, the combination of the codes varies from door to door at any given time. And each of these combinations changes every 30 seconds. So, the combination you input into this door, for instance, is valid for only 30 seconds. In the next 30 seconds, that combination changes. But there is a sequence to it, so if you master the sequence, you can guess what the next 3 codes would be. After three cycles, it changes again. I know it's a bit complicated, so I won't even attempt to explain it to you, except you care of course.' Chukwuma began to gasconade.

'No, don't worry Dad, I don't care to know.' Jane responded.

'Okay, but it's interesting anyway.' Chukwuma chipped in.

'I know. But just show me around this beautiful place and let's go for dinner. Remember I have a flight to catch.' Jane insisted.

'That's true. Let me show you the most secured thing inside this entire apartment. It's my favourite in this whole building, apart from Chika's office in all fairness; there are things, like some security gear in her office that you can't imagine.' Chukwuma says, smiling.

Jane nods as if she wasn't interested in whatever is in Chika's office. She simply wants to see this favourite place in the building and eat.

Chukwuma leads her into the kitchen and just above the wash hand basin is a light. And beside the light is a small button. Once actioned, the entire kitchen wall on the left-hand side slides left and voilà, that is CODE RED, a small cubicle that houses a chest of drawers. The Chest is protected by 100 cm of glass-clad polycarbonate bulletproof glass.

The chest is not made of wood or plastic or any of the materials that Jane is used to, but a special material which name Jane forgot immediately after she heard Chukwuma pronounce it. One thing she remembers is when his father told her that no human being born of a woman can hack the security code to open CODE RED.

'You can look at it, admire it, get angry at it, or even shoot it, but it'll keep smiling back at you.' Chukwuma boastfully says.

But there is a simple way to open it; a pear-shaped electronic device that Chukwuma had with him does the magic.

'It's just like your spouse... I know you're going to get married one day. You think I don't know about the young Emergency medicine resident, Udenna.' Chukwuma said, smiling.

'Dad, how did you know?' Jane asked, surprised at how his dad knew about Udenna.

'Well, I have eyes and I'm your father.' Chukwuma responded.

'Well, he's just a friend, a close friend actually.' Jane said, smiling.

'Yeah, we also said the same thing before we got married. You know, I and your mom were best of friends before we even thought about marriage. I had just finished my first degree in architecture while she was in her 3rd year of medicine. We met at a gospel concert and just became friends. I remember how beautiful she looked that night and the glory she exuded.' Chukwuma said, relishing the good old days.

'Alright... Alright... alright.' Jane cuts in. 'Before we start crying here, let us focus on CODE RED or BLUE or whatever colour it is.' Jane cuts in.

'Okay, I was trying to say that...' Chukwuma wipes his eyes, 'I was trying to use the analogy between a husband and his wife to illustrate how you open this place. If you unconditionally love and respect your spouse, you'll get the best from her. But if you think that by coercion, you'd force her to submit to you, you'd get only wars as a reward.' He concludes.

'Thanks, Dad, I understand. I just didn't want you to start crying all over again about the death of Mom. I'm not tired of hearing the story, but we both know that we can't do this now, and not here.' Jane calmly says, stroking her father's back.

'You're right my dear. You're very right.' Chukwuma takes a deep breath before refocusing himself on the beautiful fruit of rare ingenuity before him.

'Okay, back to CODE RED. To open CODE RED, you simply must do either of these: hit her until you are tired and worn out, yet it won't open. Or you can do this.' Chukwuma says as he licks the glass cover with the tip of his tongue.

'Daddy, you can be very crazy sometimes, you know.' Jane says cringing.

'No, I don't mean that. You can just touch the tip of your tongue with one of your fingers and then touch it at the spot where you placed the electronic key.' Chukwuma says, as if pleading innocence.

'That's unhygienic Dad. If everyone that has access to this safe box does that each time, some microorganisms will brood there. What's the essence of the licking and touching and saliva?' Jane says further cringing.

'Well, as you guys teach us in medicine, there's an enzyme in the saliva called ptyalin. Now, that spot becomes sensitive to ptyalin once you touch the electronic key. Once that happens, an input screen shows, and you can type the security code '39' and it'll open. Very simple, right?' He replied.

'How did you come up with this idea? Couldn't you have thought of using olive oil or water or vinegar or… I don't know, something liquid like milk for instance?' Jane says, still wondering how ptyalin came to her father's weird mind.

'Well, using ptyalin is a way of showing love. I couldn't have used another substance for it. That would be weirder. Anyway, there is a synthetic ptyalin on the table by your left. You use that and that's all.' Chukwuma says, smiling.

'Hmm... it's better than everyone using their saliva each time, but it's still weird.' Jane added.

'At the moment there is nothing inside CODE RED aside from the documents the FBI Director asked me to keep for him. I don't know why he couldn't wait until the official opening before asking his men to bring something in here.' Chukwuma added. 'Alright, darling. Time to go. There's nothing much left to see. There is actually, but we need to eat, and I'll take you to the airport.' he said.

As they headed for the exit of Room 39, Chukwuma tells his daughter why he thinks CODE RED can't be hacked by anyone. 'While this building was under construction, I met with the three best security code hackers in the world. I offered them one million dollars each to reveal the code to me. But after several attempts, none could hack into it. That was when I confirmed that no human can hack it. I tell you something: when you want to make a code unhackable, keep it simple. People will think the passcode is very complicated, but it's so simple that their minds won't get there. Use simple personal experiences for instance.' Chukwuma says, still visibly excited about his design.

'Well, I'm sure you didn't tell them about the ptyalin. Else that would have been easy to decode.' Jane says.

'Of course, I didn't. I mean, they were supposed to unravel the code. If I told them everything, they wouldn't be hackers anymore.' Chukwuma replied.

As they got to the exit, Chukwuma was about to tell Jane the exit code and how to understand the combination of the codes for each cycle, but Jane was in a hurry. So, Chukwuma decided to just go ahead and put the code without much talk. Jane observed but she was too tired to recall the code nor the meaning behind each letter or number that Chukwuma typed.

'I want to show you one last thing, my dear. Very quick.' Chukwuma pleads.

'Dad, we're running late, it's almost 7.40pm. By the time we get home and have a quick dinner, it'll be 8.10pm. And I must be at the airport at 8.30pm because the gate closes at 9pm.' Jane says, unhappy about the further delay.

'But your flight was meant to leave by 9pm I understood?' Chukwuma asks.

'No, the gate closes at 9pm, but my flight is at 10pm. I know that if I told you 10pm you'll take all the world to show me each detail in this Room.'

'Ok, my love. I don't want you to rush and I don't want anything to happen to my baby, so, how about I take you back myself?' Chukwuma says.

'Really? I thought you had an important meeting tomorrow morning?' She asks.

'Yes, I do, but I can reschedule it for Monday. Let me spend some time with my darling. You know I'll do anything to make you happy, right?' Chukwuma responds.

'Wow! Thanks so much, Dad. I love you. Now, I'm happy and you can show me the thing you wanted to.' Jane says, visibly excited. She had always wanted her dad to accompany her back to school in his private jet.

'And after that, we'll go have dinner at Chibyke's Delicacies. Not that your food isn't delicious… of course you know that your meals are the best, after your mom's. But I just want to take my sweet daughter out tonight.' Chukwuma adds.

'I know. I know. You and comparisons. No one cooks better than her.' Jane winks.

'Now, wait a moment. Let me get something from the car. You'll be happy with what I'm about to show you.' Chukwuma says as he heads towards his office while Jane waits inside Room 39.

'It's ok Dad, I'll be waiting.'

***

Chukwuma exits and the door closes behind him. Jane looks around the apartment observing the things that her dad had told her about the Room.

Chukwuma had left another electronic key in his office and wanted to get it. That electronic key is different from the one that opens CODE RED. Although it works similarly to the other, it serves to unlock the nine entrance doors Chukwuma talked about. Once the Opanteclaus is touched, you can activate and place the electronic key on the screen or input the code showing on the key into the screen and the door will open. It's very simple and doesn't require the use of synthetic ptyalin or saliva. And it saves you the time and stress of doing all the possible crazy combinations to get the right code to exit the Room. He intends to hand the key over to Chika on the day of the inauguration.

As Chukwuma got to his office, he noticed that the special purse where the key is stored wasn't in his office. He had mistakenly left it in the safe box in his car. So, he decided to walk straight to his car to pick it up. It was as he was headed to his car that Mbe arrived and demanded the stolen drugs and documents. While they both argued, Jane didn't know what was happening and why her dad delayed because she couldn't hear anything that was happening on the outside.

As Mbe and Chukwuma argued, what was paramount in Chukwuma's mind was the safety of his daughter. When Mbe mentioned that the items he gave to Chukwuma were drugs, Chukwuma became afraid. And when he mentioned trailing him, he knew that Mbe was aware of his daughter and would harm her if he could. So, all his tactics were geared towards making Mbe not see his daughter.

After Chukwuma was constrained to open Room 39, he purposely stood there not wanting to go in lest Mbe follows him in. He activated the security alert and raised his voice so Jane could hear him.

Initially, Jane didn't understand what was going on and was about going close to her dad when she heard another voice different from that of her father. She quickly hid behind the wall close to the entrance. So, Jane heard the rest of the conversations concerning her leaving the country, the drugs, and documents in CODE RED and how Mbe is a coward, but she did not know Mbe's name.

As Mbe shot Chukwuma, Chukwuma carefully threw the electronic key for CODE RED inside Room 39 knowing that Jane would find it. He had seen her shadow when he opened the entrance and with the eyes told her not to come close to him. As Mbe shot him, he fell outside Room 39 and the door closed.

As Mbe ran away, Jane wept sore. She had no way of getting out to help the dying father; all she had was the electronic key for CODE RED. She tried multiple times placing it on the door to see if it would open but she kept seeing 'Error. Incorrect key.' That was when it dawned on her that she would be trapped inside until someone comes to her rescue or she's able to unravel the exit code. She's been doing the latter for days now, and the progress isn't much.

CHAPTER 15

When Jane was done narrating the story of what happened, Chika was heartbroken for her sake. As Jane spoke, tears were slowly gathering in her eyes, and when Jane mentioned the fatal shooting of Chukwuma, Chika couldn't hold herself anymore. When they were done crying for the death of Chukwuma, Chika told Jane about the death of her husband, Ikem; how he supposedly drowned after his driver fell asleep on the bridge along Quib's Avenue and crashed their vehicle into a river. She expresses scepticism about that narrative as well as anger over the poor investigation conducted by the FBI so far. She tells Jane that her resolve for some time now has been to resolve this puzzle of what happened to Ike and who was responsible.

Chika's initial resolve to find out who killed Chukwuma was strengthened after Jane's story, but this time, with or without any link to Ike's case. She was ready to get Jane out of that building as quickly as possible. So, the next thing is to find the exit code. She tells Jane that they won't be using the main entrance on the first floor but will leave the Room via the third floor, which is meant to be her office.

After her sincere confession, Jane decided to be more transparent and tell her everything about CODE RED - its location and all the security details involved. Chika was very grateful for that added element of transparency and assured her that she'd do everything in her powers to bring the people that killed her father to book. When they both opened CODE RED, what they saw was exactly what Mbe and Chukwuma were talking about, which Jane eavesdropped on. It was a briefcase filled with drugs and documents. They both agree to keep the items back and focus on unravelling the exit code. Once that is obtained, they'd take the items with them while trying to find the correct combination of the code for the door.

The first thing to do is to discover the exact positions of the Opanteclaus of the nine doors. Chika already saw one in her office, through which she came in, so, she has an idea what they could look like. But identifying the nine of them won't be an easy task, no, not in a place like Room 39.

***

It was now 8am, and Chika was still inside the Room with Jane. The earlier plan of getting out of the Room in an hour has vanished into thin air, just as Dede had said. They've spent over an hour mapping out the positions of the doors. Fortunately, they found five doors using the exact points the Opanteclaus was placed on. They marked the places and began trying the combination of the codes that they had.

Chika had come up with a security code based on the discussions she had with Chukwuma, and Jane tried to recall as much as she could from the few seconds, she saw Chukwuma typing the code. They kept trying the various combinations, but none was working. As the minutes turned into hours, Chika knew that it wouldn't be long until the people that the FBI was about to send into the Room arrived. So, there was a need for a plan, a strategy. She is not alone this time, so she needs to protect herself and Jane. And most importantly, their stories need to match.

Chika's story is very easy to tell: She is the director of the Antiterrorism Unit, and this is her building where the murder took place. She came in to unravel what happened and even contributed to the FBI's search for experts to get involved. That's a credible story. A simple search of her name in any search engine would prove that what she said is true.

'How did she get the entrance code?' Simple, she is the DNI officer who has supervised the construction of the building, so it wasn't difficult for her.

'Then, how come she doesn't know the exit code?' Well, Chukwuma refused to divulge it to anyone until the official opening day; it's even in the contract the agency signed with him.

'When did she get in?' This morning; just a little over an hour ago. 'I walked in through the main entrance just like everyone else.' Chika would respond.

Essentially, all the possible questions had ready-made credible answers to them. The answers weren't going to be outright lies, else she'd be caught, but they weren't going to be completely true, else her purpose of getting into the room would be defeated.

Jane's story was a little complicated to formulate. If she said that her father is the late Chukwuma, they would ask her so many detailed questions that the answers would be so many that she could end up revealing everything that Chika was trying to keep hidden. But how does she make up a credible story that will stand for the duration of their stay in the Room?

Chika has an idea. 'How about you tell them that you're my office assistant. I brought you in to help me while waiting for them?' Chika suggested.

'And if they asked further questions like my name, where I stay, what I studied, my parents etc?' Jane quizzed.

'Well, you can tell them your true name. The rest of the information isn't necessary. You are here to assist a superior, so they should refer all their questions to me. And quite frankly, we don't have a whole week to spend here. It's just a day or two and we're out. Who has the time for long discussions and details?' Chika replied.

Jane agrees and memorises the answers. They've both gotten their stories and she was fine with the cooked-up story about being an assistant. Moreover, she wasn't ready to start telling the story of her life again to anyone. She was exhausted and just wanted to leave this 'cursed Room' and go see her dad's corpse before he's buried. Then go home to mourn for him.

The next thing to keep secret is the presence and location of CODE RED. The new entrants shouldn't know anything about its existence. And if they already knew, as Chika imagined, no one should tell them where it is located. 'If they discover it by themselves, then we'll let me attempt to force it open on their own, which they can't break for obvious reasons.' Chika added.

'Then, the last thing to maintain secret is the door that leads to the third floor. That would be the escape route, not the first-floor entrance because there will be men of the FBI, DNI and Police on standby once they exit from there. And any corrupt officials will be trailing as well to harm us.' Chika concluded. They all agreed and continued their work.

**

Getting into Room 39 for the new entrants, Kachi, Ejike and Ola wasn't much of a hassle. With the help of the DNI and FBI officials, it didn't take a while to unravel the entrance code. At 10am the main entrance on the first floor slid open and Room 39 welcomed her new explorers that will try to unlock her exit code, and she was ready to show her magnificence to them. She was ready to make them respect her and treat her with the admiration she deserves.

As soon as Chika and Jane perceived the door slide open, they quickly hid in the kitchen for fear of being seen by the officers that led the new entrants into the Room. Mbe was among the officers that accompanied them to the new building, and before they entered, in a low voice, he reminded Ola of their agreement. Then, in a loud voice, wished everyone well, hoping to see them again in three days or less. 'I wish everyone luck. For the good of everyone.' he said.

***

Talking about the agreement between Mbe and Ola, there was something that Ola has continually omitted from the encounter she had with Mbe - the promise of a huge sum of money in exchange for the drugs and documents. She has kept this promise secret from Ejike even though Ejike has already promised to take care of the hospital bill of the mom's treatment. Maybe Ola didn't believe Ejike would do it, or she wanted to still take care of the payment by herself or for some other reasons best known to her. But this secret will jeopardise the entire expedition because the promise of a huge sum of money comes at a huge price.

After the meeting with the directors at the FBI headquarters, Mbe called Ola that evening to inform her that she will be taking a special device with her into the room. That device is a sophisticated mini transmitter with a microphone that is used for special operations of the FBI. It can transmit from hundreds of kilometres and rarely gets disturbed by other frequencies. Mbe wasn't particularly sure if it'd work in Room 39, but it's better to try than allow them to be in there without monitoring what's going on inside.

***

As they got into the building, they were greeted with the usual thing everyone that enters Room 39 is greeted with - the impeccable design and attention to detail in every angle. Ejike had spent the last two days studying about the entire construction and preparing for a quick exit. With the help of the FBI and DNI, he was able to lay his hands on some of the materials Chukwuma had designed regarding the Room. So, he was aware of certain things that could be found in the Room. However, there is a big difference between seeing the design on paper and finding oneself in the physical apartment. The architectural and artistic ingenuity of Chukwuma was evident and admired greatly, albeit post-mortem by Ejike.

When Chika and Jane observed that the entrance door was shut, they pretended to be so involved with breaking the exit code. They don't want the new entrants to find them hiding, for that will generate more questions than they may be able to answer. But if they find them working on something in the sitting room, it'll be easy to tell them the story they had cooked up before they even ask.

Then, once Chika heard them chatter about the design and security installations as they walked towards the sitting room, she quickly came out to greet them and introduce herself. Jane

214

also came along and introduced herself as Chika's assistant. When they saw Chika and Jane inside the building, they were surprised. 'Who are they and why are they here?' were the questions running through the minds of Kachi, Ejike and Ola.

Chika understood their surprise and from their faces could tell they were troubled by the presence of strangers in the room. So, she welcomed them into the Room and told them that they (herself and Jane) came in earlier this morning to begin some preliminary work in the Room before their arrival. She told them that they have been able to map out about 5 different exits in the room.

While she talked, they were still suspicious of her. So, Chika went further in her transparency to tell them who she was and what she does professionally. That she is the landlord of the Room and indeed the entire building being the director of the antiterrorism unit. And that a simple check using the online search engines will reveal her identity. Ola quickly googled it while she talked and confirmed that it was so. After introducing herself and Jane as her assistant, she asks them to introduce themselves.

Ejike was the first to introduce himself among the new entrants. His principle has always been, 'when you're about to tell lies, be as close to the truth as possible, so you'd sound believable, and no one would think you're lying. And you can recall the lies any time.' So, you have figured out that Ejike told them everything about himself and who contacted him to be there. Of course, he carefully omitted the story of how their recruiters tried framing Ola up because that could reveal that their main aim is to lay their hands on the stolen drugs and documents. And neither himself nor Ola wanted anyone to know that objective.

When he mentioned that he was recruited by Mbe, Kachi took note. Kachi quickly figured out that Ejike must be there for the drugs as well. Chika already knew Ejike, so no surprises.

Ola on her part didn't say much about herself, other than she is an architect and got interested in the expedition because Ejike contacted her that he needed someone with the knowledge of architectural engineering. 'Keep it brief and wait for questions if anyone is curious to know more,' is Ola's principle of telling lies. Kachi perceived that she was hiding some details but didn't want to ask further. Chika already knew Ola as well, so no surprises.

Kachi's lies were the most stupid of all. He hadn't prepared any lies to tell. In fact, Kachi wasn't prepared for any close human interactions besides the exchange of greetings and maybe names. So, when it was his turn, he was swept off his feet and completely began talking about disjointed things.

Kachi told them that he had visited the building on a minitour with some of his students a few weeks ago. He read about this massive building in the city and thought it would be nice to exemplify some of the things he was teaching his students by bringing them to the field. 'Of a security building?' everyone asked. 'Yes, yes. You know chemical reactions are everywhere and I'm a chemical engineer too, so construction engineering, chemical engineering, just engineering and buildings and security codes and all. It's my passion. My childhood passion is to unravel the mysteries of buildings with security codes hidden in Rooms and halls and kitchens.' He said smiling.

The stories sounded insane, and the rest of the group never believed them. And when he was asked why he brought in some chemicals, he said, 'well, chemicals are needed to discover the reactions of the hands with the screen walls. And if someone has touched the screen, I could figure out the fingerprints by merely blowing on the screen and adding a bit of nitrogen.' he replied. 'Nitrogen?' Everyone chorused. 'Yeah, nitro… not really nitro… I meant hydro… hydrogen and Oxygen equal to water. So, when I add water to the screen, it purifies it, makes it clean and we can get the code and leave.'

The rest thought he was blabbing and just prayed he doesn't cause an accident that would kill everyone in the Room. Chika on the other hand took note of him. He is the only one that Chika hadn't met before now, but she was sure he had a secret agenda just like everyone else.

ROOM 39

PART FOUR

Two idiots are better than one genius

ROOM 39

CHAPTER 16

Despite the cordial approach from Chika, everyone still decided to work alone, making sure to cover up the codes they had gotten from their puzzles or experiences. While they worked or rather pretended to work, at intervals, Ola would move around in search of the location of the drugs and documents. Then Ejike will also pretend to visit the restroom but will move around the rooms and kitchen in search of any hint of CODE RED.

Kachi on his own sat at one corner of the living room pretending to resolve the exit code. He seemed to be distant from whatever the rest of the people were doing. And when Chika asked him why he isn't doing much, he simply replied that he works best when he relaxes and meditates. The only things Kachi cares about are the drugs and documents. After resolving the puzzles with the journalist, he felt that he already had the exit code, so once he could lay his hands on those stolen items, he'd disappear.

But Kachi was making a grave mistake. Everyone in the room in some measure and for different reasons wanted the same things. Ejike and Ola wanted the drugs and documents to clean up the record of Ola and help the dying mother. Chika and Jane wanted the items as a lead to discovering the assassin of Chukwuma. Kachi on the other hand wanted the drugs and documents so he could punish the Collingahs for what they did to him. So, for Kachi to even think he could lay his hands on them and quickly disappear was an illusion. It was an open secret that everyone in that room came in for reasons that transcend discovering the exit code, just that the reasons aren't known yet. No one would simply agree on that suicide mission without some personal gain. Simply put, everyone knew that everyone was hiding something.

After several hours of studying the room and of pretence, Kachi decided that it was time to set the ball rolling. He moved to a corner of the room and began mixing some chemicals just to prove to everyone that he was prepared. Unfortunately, the Room is equipped with chemical sensors that once they dictate any hazardous fumes or fire outbreak, a security mechanism is activated to neutralise the danger. And that includes the rearrangement of the exit doors and the combination of the code.

As Kachi drew his laboratory bag and took out his test tubes, in a moment, there was a rush of cold air, followed by a movement on the walls. When the noise in the walls stopped, the positions of the Opanteclaus have been altered. When Chika checked all the points, she had marked on the floor to indicate the exit, she saw that the Opanteclaus weren't there anymore. Ejike also noticed that one of the doors that he's been testing his codes on has disappeared. Everyone was mad at Kachi for bringing in chemicals into the room and warned him never to open any of those substances again until they were out of that Room.

On the table in the living Room, Ola decided to draw a map showing the places that Chika had marked on the floor. According to her, she can trace the new positions of the doors because there should be a sequence. Even if Chukwuma was a mad genius, there must be a pattern to his madness. She also thinks that by aligning the doors and using her architectural experience, the position of CODE RED can be discovered. So, while plotting her points on the map, Jane came around and they chatted. They both exchange the same false details about themselves, the only truth being that Ola loves Ejike and Jane loves a resident doctor that works in one of the hospitals in the city.

After mapping the probable points on the map, it was the moment of truth. Ola began to identify the exit points and with the help of Chika, they were able to find the seven doors out of the nine possible exit points using the Opanteclaus.

Before long it was late, and they were tired too. Chika told them that there are three rooms in the Room. So, for the night, Kachi can take one room, Ejike and Ola can take one, while she will sleep in one with Jane. They all agreed but Ola preferred to sleep in the living room instead of going to stay with Ejike. They also agree that if peradventure, someone decides to try his code at night and it works, the person should wake the rest of the people up, so they can exit together. They all agreed, but everyone knew that no one was leaving that night without the items in CODE RED. No one has time to try the exit codes tonight after the numerous trials that failed. At most, someone would go in search of those drugs and documents in CODE RED.

As Chika went to the bedroom, Ola met Jane in the kitchen and began asking some prodding questions that further revealed her intentions. She wanted to know if Jane had observed a strange construction or installation in the Room. Or if she saw any briefcase, rucksack or documents or objects hidden in some corner of the Room. Jane told her no, that she had just come in that morning with Chika to help as an assistant. When Jane asked what importance any notes or objects held for Ola, she simply said that as an architect, she can read the drawings of buildings and understand the weak points. Maybe Chukwuma left some documents in the Room that can be of help in unravelling the code. When Ola wanted to go into details of Chika's life, Jane repeated the same things that Chika had said already about herself. Ola took note that the answers were rehearsed. Jane also took note that Ola had other intentions besides the exit code.

That night as everyone went to bed, Ola got up at 2am and dialled Mbe to give him details of the operation. During the conversation, Mbe asks her if there was someone else in the Room besides the three of them that went in that morning. Ola said that there were two other people from the DNI inside the Room. Mbe was surprised at how the DNI got into the ROOM. When he further enquired, he discovered that it was the DNI Director of anti-terrorism and her assistant. Mbe wasn't surprised. He knew that Chika was the new director of the antiterrorism unit, although she was under suspension from her agency. The questions are: when did she get in and how? Mbe goes on to ask Ola if she has found the stolen drugs and documents to which she said no that they were still searching for them.

The conversation ended with Mbe reminding Ola of their agreement to drop the charges against her and the money he promised her for the mother's treatment. At the end of the conversation, Ola sneaks back into the living room. As she was returning, Kachi was also coming out from the Data centre. He had gone there to see if the stolen items were hidden under one of the installations but couldn't find anything. They both cross each other without saying a word. Kachi goes to the kitchen pretending to be thirsty, while Ola goes back to the living room pretending to sleep.

Once Kachi saw that Ola was sleeping, he began to search around the kitchen shelves and cupboards. While he was bent over looking for the drugs and documents, Chika suddenly appeared. Kachi rises pretending to be washing his hands. When Chika asked him what he was doing in the kitchen at that time, he simply responded that he was familiarizing himself with the Room. Chika stayed in the kitchen for a while until she was sure Kachi had gone back to his room. She then returns to her room to rest.

***

The second day of the expedition began with everyone waking up early to shower. Each room had a bathroom, while close to the living room were several bathrooms with bathtubs and showers. Chika woke up at 6am to have her shower. As she opened her luggage to get out some change of wear, she also got out her hoodie and jacket. As soon as her jacket was out of the luggage, Mbe's team received a signal. That was the same jacket where one of the corrupt agents had hidden a tiny audio and location transmitter. Mbe's team had been unable to locate Chika because there were many metal objects (read guns and bullets) inside her luggage. So, the metals had a negative effect on the signal transmission to their receiver.

After Ola's conversation with Mbe the previous night, Mbe had immediately alerted his team that Chika was certainly inside Room 39. They found it difficult to believe because Chika couldn't be there. When they verified that Chika's transmitter wasn't on that night, they knew that there could be some element of truth in what Ola said, seeing that Room 39 could interfere with the signals. But that morning, when the transmitter came on and they heard some noise, they were convinced that Chika was literally there.

So, Mbe decided to pay Chika's son a visit, again. They first go to Chika's house, but for the second time, there was no one around. They visited Ebuka's school but were told that he hasn't been in school for a few days now. They began to think of where her son could be and if she had friends around. They decided to visit Ebuka's favourite teacher, Miss Ifunanya, who simply confirmed what they were told at school - she hasn't seen Ebuka in days and was getting worried too.

As Chika was under the shower and Jane went to the kitchen, Ola carefully sneaked into their room. She had thought that maybe the room that Chika and Jane selected had the stolen items they were searching for. Although she didn't find what she was searching for, what she saw alarmed her greatly. She saw guns and bullets on the bed, but most importantly she recognised Chika's hoodie; the same one that Chika wore the day she photographed them at the university playground during their meeting with Mbe. Chika didn't realise that Ola took note of that, and when Ola saw it, she didn't know what to think. She quickly closed the door behind her gently and went to meet Ejike in his room.

After Ola had spoken to Ejike about what she saw in Chika's room, Ejike was convinced that they may not be the only one after the stolen items after all. He concludes that Chika and Jane knew so many things that no one knows; that they were clearly hiding something from everybody. Also, having such ammunition could mean several things that he can't really tell which is correct. Certainly, someone is not meant to leave that Room - maybe once they're able to unravel the exit code, Chika would kill them, he concluded. War was brewing, and it could turn deadly if someone doesn't give a credible and veritable explanation.

When Chika got out of the shower, she sensed that someone came into the room and left, but she wasn't sure if that was Jane or someone else. As she stepped into the living room that morning ready to try the new code, she had generated last night with Jane, she was met with angry eyes and frown faces.

Chika pretended not to have observed the countenances of Ejike and Ola sitting on the sofa. She simply goes towards Jane who was already trying out the code on one of the doors. After some minutes, Ejike and Olamma also moved towards one door and begin trying out their codes as well. For about ten minutes, whenever Chika lifted her eyes, she would be met with the angry eyes of either Olamma or Ejike. It was as though they knew the time that Chika would raise her face and they'd be waiting for her with their stares. At one point, Chika had to adjust her posture and face the opposite direction.

After about twenty minutes of apparent calmness, the gathering clouds were ready to send down rain, and it will be a heavy downpour. Chika notices that someone was walking towards them, she could sense it, but chose to ignore whosoever it was.

'We know that you have planned with the FBI to kill us once we give you the code. You're pretending to be here just for the code, but your assignment is to kill us. Otherwise, why would you have so many guns and bullets here as if you're on the war front or going on an expedition in the enemy's camp.' Ejike broke the silence.

'I told you all. I told you that this lady is no good. She told us beautiful stories of how she magically found herself inside here. How she loves us and cares about our welfare, gave us rooms to sleep and food to eat. She's evil. I know ladies like this; I've worked with many of them at the university.' Kachi added.

'What are you guys talking about?' Chika tries to feign ignorance.

'Why do you have to pretend? We already saw everything - the guns, the bullets, the knives, and even the hoodie.' Ola said.

When Chika observed that they had seen the guns and other weapons, she was embarrassed. She didn't know how to explain to Ejike and Ola that she was in the Room to unravel who killed Chukwuma. 'That's a whole complicated story to tell at this point, moreover, that could mean revealing the identity of Jane as well.' Chika thought.

'What hoodie are you talking about?' Chika asks, attempting to concentrate on the item she considers less dangerous in the list that Ola just mentioned.

'The same hoodie you wore when you spied on us at the university playground.' Ejike fumed.

'Yeah, and I saw you taking pictures of us, while you pretended to be photographing the environment.' Ola added.

'I told you all that she is a monster. The DNI is an agency of monsters.' Kachi shouted from a distance.

Jane listened as they accused Chika of plots to kill them. And when an explanation wasn't coming forth, she became apprehensive. She wondered if she hadn't made a mistake revealing all the truth to Chika. But she remembered the relationship between Chika and her father, as well as the assurances that Chika had given her and was a bit calm.

Another thing Jane isn't comfortable with is the atmosphere of suspicion in the Room and the unfriendly attitude displayed by everyone. In her opinion, everyone in there is a victim in some way, although they act as if they were in control of their lives and destiny.

So, she wanted to remove the veil; she just needed to find the perfect timing. And if bringing peace demands telling the rest of the group about the presence, location, and security code of CODE RED, she was willing to do that. After all, she has figured out that no one is ready to leave that room without the contents of that safe box.

'Alright, now I understand what you are talking about. Listen, it's not what it seems. I'm not here to kill anyone. If I wanted you all to be killed, I could have stayed outside, and when you are exiting from this place, I'd ask the officers to do that. The fact that I'm inside here shows that I'm actually interested in the code and the code only.' Chika says as she begins her explanation.

'Then, why do you have so much arsenal in your luggage? And why were you spying on us?' Ola asks, looking sternly into Chika's eyes.

'I work in the antiterrorism unit, so I need to be equipped at every moment.' Chika answers.

'Even inside your own country?' Ejike quizzed further.

'Yes, sometimes. Yes, I have to.' Chika responded.

'And the hoodie?' Ola insisted.

'On the photographs, I took at the university playground, I wasn't spying on any of you. I was just doing background checks to be sure that Mbe and the FBI select the right people for the job.' Chika said.

The moment the name Mbe exited her mouth, Ejike was infuriated, and Ola was visibly enraged. Were it not for the timely intervention of Kachi and Jane, a fistfight could have ensued.

'You are doing background checks on private law-abiding citizens who have nothing to do with terrorism? Professionals, who have their legal jobs and pay their taxes?' Kachi asks.

'That means you actually knew us before we got into this Room. And inevitably you participated in the devilish act of framing me up just to get him inside this god-forsaken Room, right? How do you all feel using my mother's disease to get me in here? How do you feel framing me up with a bag full of money, a gun and a dead man's passport?' Ola screamed.

'Madam background checks, you have no feelings whatsoever. You are monsters. You see a young lady trying to make ends meet, with a mother in the hospital for cancer, yet you want to torture her till death. Well, I knew that all of you in the military or anti-terrorism unit were demons in human flesh.

230

No feelings. No emotions whatsoever. Just forcing innocent law-abiding citizens to go on suicidal expeditions for your sake. Bastards!' Ejike adds.

As Chika heard these words, she didn't know what to say nor think. The entire story was strange to her. She had thought that she knew all of them, but really, she knew nothing about them. All she knew about them can be summarised as this: Ejike is a mathematics lecturer and Ola is an architect. She didn't do deep background checks on them and their families. And insinuating that she worked with Mbe was the worst thing she could ever say to them. It's like saying that you work with or for the devil. She regretted ever uttering those words. And to think that bringing Mbe into the picture is a lie she thought could help her escape their wrath. Now, she must dissociate herself from Mbe convincingly, and that entails saying the truth, and nothing but the truth, else Jane could explode as well.

Apart from the fact that Jane's suspicion towards Chika rose to its highest level in the last few minutes, she was further convinced that everyone in Room 39 is a victim of some sort. And she is right: Ejike and Ola are victims of Mbe's desperation to get his family from the Collingahs; Kachi is a victim of the covetous nature of the Collingahs; Jane is a victim of Mbe's murderous nature, and even Chika is a victim of Mbe although she doesn't know yet.

When Chika heard that Ola's mother had cancer, she was dumbfounded and broken... again. 'How could Mbe think of coercing someone whose mother is about to die into this? And framing her with a dead man's passport and a gun?' she thought.

After a few seconds of silence and seeing the piercing eyes of her companions, she decided to ask further questions to fully understand how Ola and Ejike were recruited. But just before the questions came out of her mouth, she reasoned within her that she owed them an explanation instead of questions.

'I know you may not believe me anymore,' she began, 'but this is the whole truth: I wasn't doing any background checks on you.' They all shook their heads in disagreement, but she continued. 'I have never worked with nor for Mbe. As a matter of fact, we work in two different agencies. If I must be very transparent, I was spying on Mbe. I had observed his movements for several months and decided to know what he is up to. Whenever there is something fishy happening in the FBI, he seems to be the first to know and first to appear at the scene. In the past, he stalked me, but I will save you all those personal details. But the truth is that I have no links whatsoever with Mbe.' She pleads.

'So, why are you here? Don't tell us that you are the DNI director and all the exit code nonsense because we know that is a cover-up for the main reason you are here!' Kachi interrupted.

'When I saw him talking to you, I felt you were his accomplices.' Chika proceeds.

'Accomplices? We are his victims.' Ola shouted.

'I felt he was recruiting you to come in here and hide any evidence that will help discover who is behind the assassination...' Chika continues.

'Assassination of who?' Ejike interjects.

'Of Chukwuma, the architect.' Jane cuts in. 'Chukwuma, the man who designed, projected and constructed this place.' Jane calmly concludes.

'We learnt of his assassination from the newspapers, but we neither know where he was assassinated nor if there's any evidence that someone is trying to hide.' Ejike says, surprised that Chika entertained such thoughts.

'Ok, I believe you.' Chika continued. 'As I said, I felt he was recruiting you to cover things up. I didn't go into details of your background - I just know that you are a researcher, and you are an architect.' Chika concludes.

'What evidence is he trying to cover up?' Ejike asks.

'Well, that brings me to the main reason why I am here. I'm here to discover and secure the evidence. We know that Chukwuma was killed at the entrance to this Room. The killer shot him fatally right there, at the main entrance. And we believe that the reason for that gruesome assassination is found here, in this Room. That is why I am here.' She said.

As Chika began talking about Chukwuma's death, Jane's eyes were filled with tears, and to avoid embarrassment, she stood up and went into the room to cry. She could not hold it anymore. Chika excuses herself to go console her, but Jane locks the door behind her and refused to open it. Chika returns to the wall to sit with the rest of the people.

'Chukwuma was my friend,' Chika continues, holding back her tears. 'I got to know him at the old building, the DNI headquarters, when he came up with the design of this place. We both got along very well, and we even discussed unofficial things as the work progressed. Such a nice man, such a genius and gentle fellow.' She adds.

'This is so sad. I'm very sorry for what happened to him. I never knew he was killed here.' Kachi said.

'Really disheartening. Please, do you know if the evidence in question has to do with drugs and reserved documents?' Ejike cuts in.

'Drugs? That's unlikely because Chukwuma wasn't into anything illicit. I mean, I knew him to some extent and there was never anything that made me suspect he is into drug trafficking.' Chika replies.

'Not hard drugs, maybe some special type of drugs. Just… ehmm… just normal drugs for diseases.' Kachi chips in.

'Maybe. I can't really tell.' Chika says, showing signs of uncertainty in her voice and visage. 'The reserved documents are more probable because he constructs buildings for intelligence and other security agencies in the world.' Chika answers.

'Why do you ask if the evidence has to do with drugs and reserved documents?' Chika asked Ejike.

CHAPTER 17

'After listening to the story of Chukwuma's death, and in the spirit of transparency, I think it's of interest to tell you that Mbe asked us to get some items for him. Yes, officially we are here for the exit code, but unofficially we were told to find the drugs and documents. I wouldn't know if this is linked in any way to Chukwuma's death, but if it'll help, you know better. Also, I don't trust Mbe after what he and his colleagues did to Ola. Those guys can kill; you can tell from merely looking at them. They even threatened me in my office when I refused their proposal.' Ejike replied.

'Yes, they told me that the only way to get my name cleared is to get those items, else I'll end up in jail and my mother will never see me again.' Ola added, crying.

'It's alright dear. Thanks for telling me. We'll find a way to get you out of this once we leave here.' Chika reassures Ola. 'Do you have any evidence that shows that Mbe asked you to steal drugs and documents out of this Room?' She asks.

'Yes, we have voice recordings of our last conversations and some photos as well.' Ejike replied.

'That's good. Do keep them. I'll also try to gather more evidence through my team once we get out of this place. You won't serve any jail term for crimes you never committed. Moreover, you're here on a national assignment. Even if he recruited you, it was the FBI that granted you access to this place officially.' Chika said, reassuring them of her support to bring Mbe and his colleagues to book.

Chika's suspicion that Mbe had a hand in Chukwuma's death was quickly becoming a conviction. Having observed Mbe since She knew Chukwuma, there are multiple reasons why he could be the assassin. And the issue of the stolen drugs and documents lays further credence to this narrative.

After the explanations and revelations, peace was restored in the Room. Although no one said it, they all knew that they had to work together to find the stolen items, escape from the Room and bring Mbe and his colleagues to book. 'Not leaving out the Collingahs.' Kachi added in his mind.

**

And speaking of the Collingahs, before they went back to work on the exit code, Chika asked Kachi if he had anything to say, maybe something to share, in the name of transparency and rebuilding of trust.

Kachi stood up and simply said, 'I will talk when the time is ripe. Let me metabolise the stories of Ola's mother and the death of Chukwuma. I don't want to talk now. But I'll talk soon.'

Chika had asked her father, Dede, to run a background check on Kachi. He was the only one Chika was surprised to see when the door of Room 39 opened because she had no idea that a third person would be part of the expedition. So, when Chika saw Kachi and listened to him tell the incredible stories that no one believed, Chika asked her father to dig deeper, 'who knows who he is and who is behind him.'

The results of Dede's investigation arrived last night, and Chika now knows who Kachi is and what his major reason for getting into the Room might be. She thought it'd help strengthen their bond if Kachi told his story by himself, instead of her doing so. Moreover, they may begin to suspect that Chika still spies on them and their families.

***

The second day of work continued with everyone trying various combinations of their codes. Although they couldn't decipher the correct combinations, there was more collaboration in the group. Chika willingly shared her codes with Ejike and Ola, while Kachi still seemed to focus on himself and his assurance of having the correct codes. 'The third day will be here in less than 12 hours. Sooner than later, Kachi will have to try those codes,' Chika told herself.

It wasn't long before the pancreatic hormones and enzymes began to demand someone to give them something before they start breaking down the deposits of glucose stored in the liver. That night, Jane offered to prepare some delicious dinner if everyone could submit what they brought into the Room. Since they were trapped in Room 39, they can as well make peace and eat together while working alone if they so preferred.

Everyone agreed and Jane made something so delicious that everyone concurred that she should simply assist in cooking while they focus on the code. And if they eventually don't make it out of Room 39, they would have eaten good meals before their demise.

'This is the best meal I've had in weeks.' Kachi says.

'Really? Then you should pay Jane to cook and send for you every day.' Ola jumps in.

'I concur. Pay Chef Jane to cook a week's meal and send it to you every week. She's truly a great cook.' Chika added, winking at Jane.

'I'll also need her culinary services.' Ejike said.

'Come on! Why do you need her when I'm here?' Ola cuts in.

'My bad. I know, but you never agree to come around to cook for us.' Ejike jokes.

'Oh, you need her to come to the house to cook for you, right?' Ola says, bopping him.

'Hahaha, not in that sense. Anyway, I know Jane understands that we all appreciate her meal.' Ejike concludes.

'But seriously Prof. Kachi, is this your best meal in a week? I mean, nothing is wrong with Jane's delicacies, but do you have someone that cooks for you - a wife, daughter or a family member?' Ola asks.

'Well…' Kachi pauses for a moment, forcing a smile, 'Well, I'm not fortunate to have any of those. I wish they were still here with me, not just for the meal, but for their company, their words, their perfumes, their warmth, their jokes, their love… just their everything.' Kachi says, pausing each time as if to emphasize how much he cherished those moments with his family.

'I once had a family,' he continues, 'a very lovely family, my strength, my happiness, my joy, my everything after God. But death, under very hurtful and harrowing circumstances, took them away from me.' Kachi said, full of tears.

As he sobs, Chika calmly moves closer to him and gently caresses his hair, 'It's alright… it's alright… it's alright. I understand how you feel. It's well.' Chika says, consoling him.

'You know, I was a very successful young man, just like Ejike here. I was doing very well, recognised nationally and internationally. In fact, the stories I told you all when we first came in was a way to disguise. I felt one of you would have recognised me given my fame, but evidently, I'm not as popular as I thought I was.' He said, smiling. Everyone giggles.

'Everything was going well for me: I married a beautiful virtuous woman, Uyom. She was my everything, and with her, we accomplished unimaginable feats in the Accademia. She conducted research work on the mitochondria while I did my things in chemical engineering. With her understanding of biology, we were able to build a biomedical laboratory that attracted other young talented researchers. Things were really rosy until that … that… terrible morning when a drunk driver knocked her car.' Kachi sobs, holding himself from tearing up in front of everyone.

'I thought the pains were much, but with a young daughter to raise, I had to be strong. I needed to be strong for her and myself because Uyom, my strength, was gone. Nnenna, my daughter, grew to be a fantastic young lady, taking all the beautiful and most virtuous qualities of Uyom. But death felt like it hadn't tormented me enough. So, after years of studies and accomplishments, Mr Death came and took her at her prime as well. And I even contributed… I was just a stupid but caring father.' Kachi weeps, wiping his tears with the table handkerchief, and Jane massages his shoulders to relieve his heart.

'After her death,' Kachi continues, 'I dedicated myself wholly to developing drugs that would help cancer patients lead a normal pain-free life. I tried several times, but nothing was working. And when my sponsors saw that nothing tangible was coming out, many of them withdrew their funds from my laboratory. I was convinced of a particular drug that I was working on... I was sure of its potential, so I continued and kept searching for funds.'

'May God curse that day when I met a Venture Capitalist. I have always wanted financiers that don't dictate what I should or shouldn't do. I've always preferred funds from people who love science and appreciate my work. This one seemed interested in my work and promised me funds beyond our request. And he truly delivered in that aspect. But when he saw that the drug had a very potent euphoric effect, he manifested his true colour.'

'He was from the Collingahs, and I didn't know; that was my first mistake. I never wanted to synthesise a drug that produces a euphoric effect that is twenty times that of heroin, but he insisted. When I refused, he destroyed my laboratory and stole the drugs and reserved documents detailing all the steps required to synthesise the drugs. They carted away my life work and threatened me with a video. I don't know how they got it.' Kachi paused.

While he spoke, the whole table was in tears. It seems like each story is more saddening than the previous one. They were just a group of people carrying heavy burdens and wounds that haven't been healed completely. Room 39 seemed to have attracted the externally happiest but internally saddest people living in Pirro. Had the colours settings of the Room not been disabled, it'd have turned thick black on hearing each of these stories.

'Thank you, everyone,' Kachi says while trying to stop himself from crying further.

'Wow! I haven't let out so much burden from my eyes in a very long while,' he heaves. 'I think it's therapeutic. One should cry occasionally just to clean one's eyes and offload the burdens in one's heart.' Kachi says, smiling and wiping his face.

'Anyway, the juice or substance of my entire discussion is this: there's a rumour that those drugs and documents were stolen from the Collingahs by some corrupt FBI agents as they were transported to a safe place. Rumour also has it that the drugs may have been brought into this Room. I don't know how true that rumour is because I've searched and searched but couldn't find any drugs or documents in here. The truth is that I decided to participate in this expedition because I wanted to lay my hands on those items and use them to punish the Collingahs. I want to frustrate their plans to flood the market with potentially harmful drugs that would cause such a terrible disaster that the recent opioid crisis would look like a joke.' Kachi concludes.

'Then, those drugs must definitely have been stolen by Mbe and his corrupt colleagues, no doubts.' Ola said, convincingly.

'Hmmm... no wonder Mbe said something like, *'when the lives of your family are at stake, you'd do anything to save them'* or something similar.' Ejike added.

'That means that Mbe stole the drugs and documents, and maybe the Collingahs threatened or kidnapped his family members. Now, he wants the stolen items so he can redeem them.' Kachi added.

As he said this, Chika looked at Jane and resolved in her heart that those drugs and documents will never get into the hands of Mbe nor the Collingahs. It was clear that Mbe must have stolen the items from the Collingahs and is either desiring to send them back to the Collingahs or wants to start a drug business himself.

Just as everyone was done consoling Kachi, Jane felt it was time to disclose her real identity. She thought it was the perfect timing she had been waiting for.

'Since it's confession time, let me just tell everyone that my name is Jane and I am the daughter of Chukwuma, the architect that was killed. I was actually in this Room when he was killed.' Jane began to cry as she narrated the story of how her father was killed. Everyone in the Room had no doubt who the prime suspect was at this point. All fingers point towards Mbe. One person who for selfish reasons seems unsatisfied with the amount of bloodshed he has caused.

As the unarranged therapy session was going on, Ola stood up, went towards her bag, grabbed the device with which she talks with Mbe and headed towards the bathroom. When she got to the bathroom, she called Mbe, who immediately picked up the call, ready for updates on the drugs and the documents.

'I called to tell you to go and rot in hell.' Ola screamed. 'You and the Collingahs and your family and everyone one of your corrupt colleagues. I don't care what you intend to do with the false evidence you planted in my house. I have a recording of your confession and photographs of you. You can't do me anything. And quite frankly I don't care anymore. It's either I die, or you die. But before I die, I'll make sure the world gets to know who you and your corrupt colleagues truly are. I'll send all the recordings of you that I have to all the media houses in the country. And for the drugs and documents, forget them. Although we haven't seen them, even if we do, you will neither see nor smell them. You're done, Coward! And your money can perish with you... Coward!' Ola shouts and hangs up.

As she talked, Mbe tried to threaten her, but she wouldn't budge. Chika and Ejike stood a few metres away listening to her conversation with Mbe. When she was done, Chika and Ejike didn't say a word. Although they were shocked to see that someone among them was almost acting as a spy, they were pleasantly surprised at Olamma's boldness and the words she told Mbe.

***

After a pause of about twenty minutes where everyone essentially felt relieved for sharing their most intimate worries and pain, Chika thought that the time was ripe to tell everyone of the existence of CODE RED.

'Please, let everyone come. I want to show you all something. Please come.' Chika beckons with her hand.

They all stood and followed Chika to the kitchen. Jane sensed what was about to happen and was so glad that it's happening; this was the perfect timing she has looked forward to since they got into the Room. As they got to the kitchen, Chika asked Jane to show them CODE RED.

'I know you all will be surprised,' Chika began, 'Well, you shouldn't be. I know you all understand why we decided to keep it secret until we understood everyone's intention for being here. I came in here with the desire to know who killed Chukwuma, but more importantly who killed my husband. But after staying with Jane for an hour, I understood that I was being selfish, using others' misfortunes for my gain. So, I dropped my ambition. My only desire is to know who killed Chukwuma and make him pay. If that eventually leads to the discovery of what happened to my husband, that will be great. But if it doesn't, that will be fine as well. He will receive justice in due time.' Chika said, not showing any signs of breakdown.'

For the first time, they all got to know that Chika mysteriously lost her husband. They proceeded to see the stolen items and afterwards went back to the sitting room to work.

One of the major reasons for coming into Room 39 has been solved, the next thing is to unravel this exit code. Now, they can concentrate, putting their expertise into use. Chukwuma's head can't be better than the heads of five great people put together, for even two idiots are better than a genius. And they weren't idiots.

That night no one slept. It was as if the session of confession and transparency reinvigorated everyone. Not to forget that Jane's food tasted out of this world.

Ejike decided to unleash his latent music talent, not in singing though, but in the choice of the right genre of music needed at such moments when perfect neuronal synapses and hypersensitivity of all the sense organs are needed. Simply put, they all needed to concentrate on unravelling this code, and what more than a playlist of great classical music is needed. And one more thing: Room 39 had the best acoustics ever. This is the biggest project Chukwuma had ever done, and he truly spent his time in making every part of this building superb, and every part of Room 39 celestial.

As Tchaikovsky's The Sleeping Beauty played, the Einstein in Ejike was resurrected. With eyes half-closed, he swirled his head as if he was under the influence of something Kachi knows well. Intermittently, Ejike could be seen slowly gliding close to the wall, the living room, and the Data centre. The more he moved, the more he solved the puzzles. If Chika's Pastor were to be present, he would have exorcised him... certainly. But he wasn't around, and Chika is inexperienced in casting away demons. And quite frankly, provided that Ejike solved the puzzles, Chika was fine. And to cast away 'this demon' simply requires turning off the Beethoven or Chopin or Brahms or Verdi or ... what's the name again? Tchaikovsky and this whole transcendental experience would end.

As the music played and Ejike was able to solve the puzzles at a greater speed and an ethereal precision, Jane was reminded of what her dad, Chukwuma had told her the day he showed her CODE RED. 'It's just like your spouse, if you treat her with love and respect, she'll give you her best.' So, as the music played, Jane was convinced that Room 39 listened and loved the atmosphere. Had they not deactivated the lightning that showed emotions, she was convinced everywhere would be pink right now. There was love in the room and Room 39 could feel it.

Ejike was able to re-solve all the puzzles at his disposal. There were still a few puzzles left, and Kachi knew that his time to get into action was around the corner; he knew that he had what no one else had in the Room - the unpublished puzzles.

While the music played, Olamma took out her map once again and wanted to discover the rest of the doors. With some help from Chika, they found the Opanteclaus of the other two doors. All the doors were now completely mapped out. What is left are a few numbers or letters of the exit code and the right combination, and they'll be out of the Room.

All the while Kachi was very busy eating apples on the sofa while going through those reserved documents containing the chemical reactions he had written. He was still interested in leaving the Room, but as you know 'he had the codes.'

When The Nutcracker by Tchaikovsky began to play, Kachi felt it was the perfect time to enter the scene in grand style.

'Shut up young woman abi man! You're disturbing the serenity of this environment. What is wrong with you? Do you think that you're the only one interested in finding a way to leave this god-forsaken building? We've tried all your suggestions but none of them worked. Get out of that place before I spend the last ounce of strength in me to crack you down.' He barked. (Remember chapter One?)

Everyone was surprised, but Kachi smiled and winked at Chika to signify that he was joking.

'You see old man, were it not that I respect the few grey threads on that bald skull, I'd have smacked you like a child.' Chika retorted, laughing. And the whole Room burst out laughing, including Kachi.

***

It was now 10am and they had spent 14 hours trying to unravel the exit code. Although they were close, a few letters and numbers were missing. Ejike has just finished with the puzzles he had and was working with his device to see if he can generate the missing parts by following the pattern of the ones he had solved. Ola was testing the Opanteclaus on the doors. Jane was trying Ejike's codes. Chika was trying her code and helping Olamma.

'Hey Jane, try these codes. They should work, trust me.' Kachi said, *con l'aria di un saputello*.

'How did you get the codes?' asked Ola

'Well, the truth is that I was recruited, not by the FBI but by the Journalist.' Kachi answered.

'You mean Kean, the online journalist?' Ejike asked.

'Yes, Mr Kean, the online and offline journalist.' Kachi replied. 'Prior to meeting the FBI, I contacted him to know if there were other puzzles that Chukwuma sent to him which he hadn't published. Initially, he was reluctant, but after I told him my story, he was willing to share the puzzles with me. After sharing them with me, he deleted them because the FBI was after his records. So, we both solved the puzzles and generated the security code in Jane's hands.'

'Wow! Interesting story.' Jane says as she turns to input the code.

'Hey Jane,' Kachi calls, 'Kean is really interested in finding and punishing whoever killed your father. He refused to publish the remaining puzzles after he learnt of your father's death. He thought that the murderers could lay their dirty hands on the puzzles and use them to cover up their crime. He truly loves your dad and he's rooting for us.' Kachi concludes.

'Alright, thank you. I hope I get to meet him when we're done from here.' Jane says.

'Sure, I will arrange for that if you want.' Kachi concurs. 'Now, let's try the code. If they don't work, then we might be doomed.' Kachi concludes.

Chika asks Jane to choose a door different from the main entrance on the first floor. That way, if it worked, they won't find themselves unprepared in front of FBI and DNI agents that you don't know if they're part of Mbe's team or not.

Everyone held their breath when Jane was inserting the code, they all prayed and hoped this code works. That would be a perfect ending to this drama that began years, months, weeks or days ago depending on who you are in the Room.

Jane inserted all the letters and numbers in the code, and they were all accepted, and a green light showed, but just as they were expecting the door to open for them to jump in excitement, there was a blink, two white spaces appeared. They were surprised, thinking of what those signify - another set of code or a fingerprint or ptyalin or… what?

While they pondered, Jane suggested that they try the ptyalin, maybe that's what is required. They got the ptyalin and applied it on the spot but there was no change. Chika tried her fingerprint, but it didn't work either. They also used the pear-shaped electronic device meant for CODE RED, but nothing changed. Instead of opening it, it showed an error message. When the error message cleared, the screen returned to its default level. They tried reinserting the same security code but this time it showed that the combination is wrong.

CHAPTER 18

At this point they were tired and confused; they hadn't slept for over 14 hours because they wanted to unravel the code. And it was the third and last day they were meant to be in Room 39. Before they decided to go have brunch, Ejike asked them to give him some minutes to see if he could generate multiple combinations of Kachi's code with his machine. That would save them time and multiple trials.

In less than 3 minutes, Ejike's generated combinations were put on trial on 4 different doors within thirty seconds. Two of the doors showed the green light, confirming that at any given instance, the 9 doors use different combinations of the same code. So, the code is fixed, but the combinations vary. Seeing that the combination changes after 30 seconds, they have time to input three combinations on each door. The only thing left is understanding what the white spaces that show after the green light signify. That holds the key to their exit.

After the combinations were confirmed, Ola asked the group if she could change the entrance security code into the Room from inside. Afraid that Mbe or his cohorts might come into the room since the entrance security code is known, they decided to change it. Instead of 39 (iri ato na itoolu), they changed it to 38+1 (iri ato na asato na otu). This way, no one can come into the Room from outside and they'll have all the time to plan their moves in case they were able to unravel the exit code.

Now secure in the Room, they decided to take a couple of hours to eat and rest. It was already past 2pm and they were quite hungry. Jane couldn't repeat her culinary magic because she was worn out just like everyone else. Thanks be to God because last night's meal was so much that the leftover could serve for two mealtimes. So, they warmed the food to eat. While the food warmed, Chika's phone rang. It was Dede calling.

***

Mbe's men had visited Dede's house last night. Mbe had remembered that Chika's parents lived in the outskirts of the city, some kilometres away from the ever-busy Pirro's Lane, in the woods. So, he sent his men to kidnap Ebuka.

When they arrived, Dede was well prepared for them. He asked Ebuka to go underground, and locked him there, while he positioned himself in the hut built a few metres away from the main house. When Mbe's men entered, the cameras captured them, and from his control room in the hut, Dede neutralised one of the men in the house. Then, he shot another that was roaming around his hut. The last one shot and almost hit Dede were it not for the ballistic helmet Dede had on.

Dede relished his moment as a combat soldier on the battlefield of many countries around the globe. But he is old now and doesn't have much strength to fight. So, when the last corrupt agent wanted to engage in a fistfight, Dede obliged. But instead of fighting with his fist, Dede drew a knife and slit his femoral and carotid arteries. He then closed the bleeding arteries with his fingers and asked him to confess who sent them and why. The dying man confessed that Mbe sent them to kidnap Ebuka. Afterwards, Dede allowed him to go in peace… I mean, to return to his Creator in peace.

After the call with Dede, Chika was furious with Mbe and almost called to warn him about his moves, but Kachi dissuaded her, warning that it may be counterproductive doing so. Although they were all mad at Mbe, they felt it was best to pretend as though they knew nothing about what he was doing outside.

Ola tells them that Mbe's true plan is to kill all of them once they exit the Room, beginning with Jane who was an eyewitness to the death of her father, Chukwuma. Then Chika, who now knows the truth concerning the death of Chukwuma. Then, of course, Ejike. She wasn't sure about Kachi's fate but seeing he is inside the Room with them, it's unlikely that Mbe and his colleagues would leave him alive. Her fate was already decided.

***

During lunch, they kept thinking of what the blank space could represent. It was amid the contemplations that Kachi made a statement that triggered off something in Chika's mind.

At some point during their discussion, they touched on the kidnap attempt again and how Dede defended Ebuka. It was at this point that Kachi remarked that men, no matter how old they are, will always risk their lives for the person or thing they love. Just like Chukwuma who risked his life to save his daughter Jane.

Once Kachi made that remark, something was triggered in Chika and she remembered what Dede told her the night she left the house for Room 39, *'men always love to use the names of people and things they love as their password.'*

So, Chika immediately asks everyone to come to the wall. An idea has just dropped in her mind on what that blank space could represent and what they need to input. She tells them that Chukwuma, being a romantic man, may have used the names, birthdays, or birthplaces of people he loves so much. Or he may have used names of places where he has lived. Or his favourite sports games. So, they'll be trying any of these possible solutions. If any of them work, then they have the complete exit code, and they're ready to leave the Room.

Ejike immediately gets his device ready to generate combinations of the security code for the doors. He inputs the code that Kachi had brought and sets the machine to work. Meanwhile, in the background was The Sleeping Beauty. In less than a minute, they had the 9 combinations, and Ola, Jane, Chika and Kachi tried them immediately, paying attention not to do so on the main entrance on the first floor. Three out of the four doors accepted the combinations as correct.

Once that was done and the blank space showed, Chika quickly asks Jane for her birthplace, just the abbreviation in letters. She tried it but it didn't go, so she asked for her birth year. That didn't go as well, rather an error message was displayed. Chika asks for her mother's birthplace and birth year, but those didn't go either.

When those guesses didn't work, Jane asks Chika to try her data - birthplace and birth year. Every other person was surprised at that suggestion, except for Jane and of course

252

Chika. They've come to know that Chukwuma and Chika were close, but not so close to the point that he would use Chika's birthplace or birth year as part of the code. Chika calmly inserts her birthplace, but an error message appears. Then Jane asks her to use her birth year instead. The moment she did that, the door threw itself open. And immediately, the famous song by George F. Handel began to play in Room 39.

Hallelujah! Hallelujah! Hallelujah! Hallelujah! Hallelujah!
Hallelujah! Hallelujah! Hallelujah! Hallelujah! Hallelujah!
For the Lord God Omnipotent reigneth
Hallelujah! Hallelujah! Hallelujah! Hallelujah!

Immediately the door opened, the excitement in the Room could not be contained; they all exclaimed with indescribable joy as the door moved sideways. Fortunately, the door that opened is the same door that leads to the third floor, to Chika's office. Everyone wanted to have a peep of how outside the Room looked but they soon advised themselves to the contrary lest they be caught unprepared by the guards. It felt as though they've been indoors for decades, not seeing the sun nor any stars.

They quickly let the door close as they got in to plan on the best strategy to exit the Room. They are all aware that Mbe and his corrupt cohorts will surely come after them, either at the main entrance or once they leave the building. Their lives were at risk and unfortunately, they can't differentiate between the true and false FBI agents.

Since the door was securely closed, they soon excogitate a plan. The first agreement is that they won't go out together through the main exit. Chika and Jane weren't in the original group that the DNI and FBI brought in. Moreover, Chika is still under suspension from the DNI, so seeing her there would be bad for her career and would undermine the integrity of their national service as well. The presence of Jane would raise more questions than provide answers.

So, Chika and Jane would leave the Room at 4am through the third floor. That way, Chika can also protect Jane in case of an attack by the guards. In any case, everyone in the Room would be given a firearm by Chika; she had more than enough for an army of soldiers.

The second plan had to do with the custody of the drugs and documents. Also, in this case, the items won't be kept by the same group of people, lest the corrupt agents cart them away at once. So, they all agreed that Kachi will keep the drugs while Jane will keep the reserved documents since they were the least known or at risk of being killed by Mbe and his men.

The third plan was the time of departure. Since Chika and Jane will leave at 4am, Kachi, Ola and Ejike will leave at dawn the next day to permit Chika and Jane to escape. This would be the fourth day.

***

Since the agreement with the FBI and DNI directors was for three days, some agents were assigned to open the entrance at 4pm on the third day. But, when the FBI agents came to the Room to unlock the door for them to exit, the Room wasn't opening; their entrance code wasn't unlocking the door. When the FBI agents tried contacting Ejike and Ola, their phones weren't reachable. This was done on purpose by Ejike and Ola to allow them time to plan properly before exiting the Room.

When they were done planning, they decided to contact the Directors' office. Through Chika, they were able to speak with the apex offices directly. They informed the Directors that while conducting numerous trials on the door, it's possible that they inadvertently altered the entrance code. So, now they must find both the entrance and exit codes, and that would require between 12 hours to 24 hours. They promised that they were close to the results and the FBI shouldn't attempt using earthquakes or any other violent means to open the door, else the entire building would collapse. Having settled this, they all go to rest for a few hours before the D-Hour of departure arrives.

***

At 2am, they all woke up, well-rested and ready to face the day. Chika anyway hadn't slept at all, or maybe for just an hour. She's used to going for days without sleep during her missions, so it was normal for her to spend the night planning and strategizing. She knew that this is the most crucial part of the game; when you feel comfortable and safe, that's when the enemy strikes. Just like the enemy did when she travelled with her squad to Zumkin to capture Selence. She doesn't want to lose anyone and would have preferred to escape at 4am with all of them through the third floor. But leaving in two groups was a better option.

When the others woke up, Chika had arranged their firearms, prepared breakfast and gotten all her things ready. They all greet one another and rehearse their plans: Chika and Jane were to leave the Room. Once they have gotten to safety, Chika would keep Jane with Dede and return to the building at 10am to see that the rest exit the building in safety. She would call to notify the FBI and DNI that there was possible infiltration among them.

At 3.30am, it was time to say a short prayer. Usually, Chika would appoint one of her men to pray before leaving for the enemy's camp, but none of the people in the Room understands warlike prayers because they were all civilians. Anyway, she decided to ask Ejike, the transcendental brother, to pray for them and for the rest of the expedition. Ejike prays the much he understood, thanking God for the feat they had achieved and asking God for protection as they exit the building today.

After the prayers, it was time for Ejike to perform his magic and generate the possible combinations. Chika would then try them on the exit door she'll be using with Jane and that would be it.

Since classical music had worked the previous times, Ejike quickly started his playlist once more. In a minute the combinations were generated and one of them matched Chika's exit route. They all hug each other, and Jane and Chika leave through the door, while the others wave at them almost nostalgically. Ejike, Kachi and Olamma went back to the rooms to arrange their belongings and get ready for whosoever will cross that door at 10am to get them.

***

Chika decided to leave behind her luggage and other things that could be burdensome to her. The only exceptions were all the guns and bullets that she didn't leave for Kachi, Ejike and Ola. Before they left the Room, Kachi gave them a small container of corrosive chemicals. According to him, they could be used to dissolve any obstacle they meet along the way. Chika and Jane mounted the same silent mini elevator that brought Chika

256

into Room 39, and on the third floor, they entered Chika's office. There, Chika explains to Jane the direction they'd follow to get out of the building - it's the same route she took when she got into the building a few days ago.

During their sojourn in Room 39, the tracking device that was attached to Chika's jacket by Mbe's colleague worked sparsely. So, although Mbe knew that they were still inside the building, he couldn't tell what they were discussing nor their exact position in the building. Mbe's team was positioned outside the new building for the Antiterrorism Unit on the morning of the third day. They were prepared to infiltrate the group of agents that will receive Kachi, Ejike and Olamma as they exit Room 39. But after the call was made to the directors of the FBI and DNI by Ejike and Ola, the exit and consequent reception were frozen until the next day, hopefully.

At 4.07am, there was a signal on the monitor of Mbe's men. The signal was coming from the building, and on a close look, they observed that it's the device that was attached to Chika's jacket. On a closer look, they noticed that the person was moving. They quickly alert Mbe who drove speedily to the building premises.

As Chika was leaving the Room, she had worn the same jacket that had the tracking device on it. So, as they tracked her, through the microphone, they could hear some gunshots and fistfights, but couldn't tell if Chika was alone or not, as she only talked by signs with Jane.

Chika recalled the positions of the guards, so she made sure she neutralised them before asking Jane to come forward. She rarely used guns so as not to attract other guards towards her direction. Moreover, they were her men doing their official duties, so they weren't enemies that should be killed. The only thing she made sure of was that they were incapacitated for the time needed for them to escape the building.

They were able to get to the office window through which Chika had entered on the night of her arrival. As they tried to climb down, a guard shot Chika on the left arm. Chika was injured but as Jane checked the injury, she saw that it was superficial. She tears a piece of her cloth and ties it around the wound to stop the bleeding. Mbe and his cohorts continued to track Chika, and once the shots were fired, they knew exactly at what corner of the building Chika was.

Chika and Jane slowly climb down the window and neutralise the guard at the corner of the building. As they moved towards the bush path that leads to the place where Chika parked her vehicle, a guard almost shot Jane from behind. Chika heard a shot behind her and immediately was frozen, she feared that Jane had been killed. But as she turned to check, she saw a guard fall behind her.

When she looked up, she saw a young man with an eye mask walking behind her. As Chika drew her gun and looked on to identify the person, Jane ran towards him and hugged him tightly. Chika was confused.

'Who is he and what is he doing here? And how did he know that we are here?' Chika asks Jane.

'He is my fiancé. His name is Udenna. I called him. I'll tell you everything later. Let's go.' Jane signals Chika.

While they talked, Mbe approached and shot at them but missed his target. They quickly ran behind a vehicle parked close to them and hid.

'Hello, Madam director. Why leave at night when everyone is sleeping. Are you the biblical evil lady who doesn't come close to the light because her deeds are evil?' Mbe teases, laughing hysterically.

Chika ignores him and searches for a place to hide Jane and Udenna. As they try to turn, Mbe shoots again, and again. They wait for a moment and skip towards another vehicle a few metres away. When Mbe got to the first position and couldn't find them, he began to search under the vehicles with his men.

'Must we play this hide-and-seek game? Why not give me the drugs and documents and let everyone go their way?' Mbe asked. 'You are a beautiful lady, and I don't want to harm you. I mean, I could have done that a long time ago, but I decided not to do it. I must admit that you made me jealous, the way you were always going to see that old fool called Chukwuma. But it's ok,' he continued, 'I've taken him out of the way now, so we can be together. Just give me those items you took from that Room and we're fine.' He said, searching carefully for the new hideout of Chika and crew.

When Mbe mentioned Chukwuma, Jane was moved with anger. She wanted to rush at him and kill him if she could, but Udenna held her back. She fumes and calms down, patiently waiting for when she would have the chance to offload her wrath on Mbe.

As Mbe slowly approached to shoot Chika again, a shot was fired at him. The bullet misses its target and Mbe quickly runs into hiding. The shooter comes closer and shoots at him again and he runs farther away from Chika. Then the shooter comes closer and gently comes behind Chika and asks her to take off her jacket. Chika was a bit confused initially because the voice sounded familiar, but the shooter had an eye mask just like Udenna, so she couldn't identify him.

The shooter observes that she wondered who he was and why she should take off the jacket, and simply whispered, 'It's me Nnem. It's Ikem.' Chika almost fainted, she couldn't believe her ears and eyes. It was still dark, but Ikem looked very healthy, just the stark opposite of a dead man. She wanted to scream for joy, but Ikem covered her mouth with a gentle kiss and told her that it's not over yet.

'There's a tracking device with a microphone hidden inside your jacket. That's why I asked you to take it off.' Ikem whispers.

Chika quickly takes off her jacket and hands it over to Ikem, as Jane and Udenna enjoy the whole beautiful drama, albeit in chaotic scenery.

'Just protect Jane and Udenna, and of course, your precious self. Let me get this man. I'll be back in a moment. And I'll tell you everything. Ok?' Ikem says, smiling.

Chika was so excited seeing Ikem; it was as if someone had injected 50 years of good life into her. She couldn't wait until everything was settled to ask Ikem what happened and where he's been all these years.

Ikem takes the jacket and runs away while shooting in Mbe's direction. He wants to use the microphone to lure Mbe in an opposite direction. Mbe checks his tracking device and sees that the signal has shifted to a different location. He follows the signal, shooting and talking senselessly.

***

Ikem had received information from a reliable source that Chika was in the building. He was also told that Mbe was tracking his wife via a microphone mounted device to kill her. So, he found a way to tap into the frequency of Mbe's men. And through their monitor, he was able to locate Chika.

After running some distance, Ikem dropped the jacket behind a vehicle and moved a few metres away from it. One of Mbe's cohorts approached with his tracker and saw that the jacket was on the floor. As he tries to turn, Ikem asks him to drop his gun if he doesn't want to drop dead. This agent was part of the corrupt team that attempted to kill Ike at the bridge. He drops the gun and turns to see who was aiming at him. When he saw Ikem, he smiled, trying to portray courage and fearlessness.

Ike comes close carefully and kicks his gun away. As Ikem prepares his gun and sets to pull the trigger, Mbe appears from behind him and asks him to drop the gun too. Ikem was frozen, he had imagined a different end to this entire story. He had spent years preparing for this moment, just for him to have the same person who tried to kill him at the bridge point his gun to his head.

Ikem slowly drops his gun, raises his hands, and turns. As Ikem slowly turns, he finds Mbe staring sternly at him. Mbe asks him to take off the eye mask slowly. As he did, Mbe was surprised at who was standing before him. He couldn't believe that Ike survived the bridge incident after the car fell into the river.

He shrugs his shoulders and says, 'Well, I thought you had died, man, but evidently, I was wrong. How did you survive?' Mbe asks as if he was interested in the answer.

'Well, God helped me. It wasn't my time to die.' Ike said, smiling and gesticulating with his shoulders and hands.

Mbe comes close to Ikem, kicks away his gun and carefully searches his body for any other weapon while Ikem responds.

'Fair enough. We'll find out if God has decided to call you back home today. You believe in God and destiny, right? Ike, the born-again Christian?' Mbe mocks him.

'Well, we'll soon find out. If He delivered Daniel from the Lions' den, I don't think your gun is more dangerous than the claws and teeth of lions.' Ike replies.

'Ok, I agree, my gun is not dangerous.' Mbe erupts again in hysterical laughter, before turning serious. 'But I'm going to shoot you in the head to see if He will protect you. Then, I'll shoot you everywhere else. But let's just start from the head as an experiment, ok?' Mbe said sarcastically.

As he readied his gun to shoot, he heard a voice from behind intimating him to drop his weapon. Mbe recognises that voice and knows that if he drops his weapon, it is over for him. So, he tries to talk Chika away from shooting immediately.

'Your husband, Ike, is a very nice man, handsome and kind-hearted. But he's a very lucky man too, I would say, to have a beautiful young lady like you.' Mbe begins, still facing Ikem. 'Truly, I didn't want to kill him. I just wanted to frighten him a bit to stop his project to spy on us. That's all. But he wanted to show that he is good with his software or whatever you call it, thereby spoiling my business, our business essentially. Well, he had to go. A little sacrifice to protect our business, you know?' Mbe said.

'Director Chika, I know you understand me,' he continued. 'We're both warriors, not this guy who is a bloody civilian that the DNI employed as a technician from the university and now he's the boss while we're still trying to work ourselves up the ladder. He sits in his office and has all the comfort while we deal with the bad guys outside. Anyway, it seems you're having a fair share of promotion as well.' Mbe pauses.

While Mbe talked, Chika only prayed that he doesn't pull the trigger on Ikem. She was prepared to shoot in that case, but how fast can she be. Mbe is a professional killer disguised as an FBI officer, he knows the tricks. Chika also knows the game quite well, but her mind was so clouded with Ikem. She can't afford to lose him now, after years of tears and sacrifice. When Mbe delayed shooting, Chika understood that Mbe's target was different this time – 'if I can't have you, no one else would'.

'Hey Chika, leave this guy alone. Let him join his Creator in heaven while we live a beautiful life that our creator has given to us here on earth.' As he makes these final sentences, he sharply turns around to shoot Chika.

Chika understood his intentions all the while but wanted to hear him voice out those words that confirm his involvement in what happened to Ikem. As Mbe turns to shoot her, she pulls her trigger and shoots his pectoral girdle. Ikem quickly pulls a knife that was tucked away in his left wrist and directs it at Mbe's armpit. The knife stuck under Mbe's armpit and lacerated his axillary nerve.

When the other officer saw the unfolding drama and attempted to pick up his gun to shoot Ikem, Udenna quickly blocked him. 'No, no, no, no. If I, were you, I wouldn't touch it.' Udenna hints as he draws near and picks the gun.

***

When Jane saw that Mbe's arms were out of use, she came out of hiding and in grand fashion emptied her barrel on Mbe. Fortunately for Mbe, they were all directed at his right patella (kneecap). When Mbe fell, she came close and shot the last bullet on the left patella. Her precision was so good that Ikem was wowed. Chika simply told him that Jane is almost a doctor, so she knows where she aims at. While everyone looks on amazed, Jane comes close, rips Mbe's jacket apart and ties the bleeding parts of his body.

'You are not going to die so quickly, coward. Not now. You will live to enjoy all the pains you've caused everyone. You will go to jail and pay for your crime...Coward!' Jane concludes, re-echoing the same name her father had called Mbe the night he was killed. She stands and walks towards the waiting car placid as if what just happened never took place or took place in a dream.

Udenna quickly calls the emergency unit that someone was dying and needed immediate help. And in a minute, they arrived at the scene.

Hmmm... alright. The truth is that I invented the last three paragraphs above to underline how angry Jane was. And what she had thought to do whenever she met the man who killed her father. She would have loved to empty her anger and frustration on the man who fatally shot her dad for something he wasn't involved in. She would have loved to empty her barrel on the man who made her an orphan. Oh, how she would have loved to strangulate him while looking into his fixed enlarged pupils but recalling the pool of blood her father died in! That would have been a good ending to the torment this same man has caused several families.

But the moment Jane saw that Mbe's arms were out of use, she felt an unusual sense of pity towards him. An unusual type of love that only God and Scriptures can explain. It's a type of thing you can't describe. Do you know that type of love that makes you feel bad for your enemies? That type of love that is well explained by Jesus in the Bible, but which we rarely see in the world today? Yeah, that's what Jane felt when she saw Mbe. She was weak and began to cry looking at the man that took her dad away from her.

The only words she could mutter after wiping her tears were, 'I... I love... I love you. Despite all that happened, I... I...' Jane breathes deeply, 'I forgive you. I truly forgive you from the depth of my heart.'

Mbe was petrified hearing this young lady say those words. For a moment, the pain from the shot on his pectoral girdle seemed inexistent. He felt both hot and cold at the outburst of such love from Jane, that he began to weep.

Chika was standing, dumbfounded as Jane mouthed those words. She couldn't help but cry with her. Ikem couldn't hold himself any longer. He simply reached over and hugged Jane. While they cried, Dede appeared from a distance and asked them to jump into the vehicle because he wanted to go home to sleep. Dede arrived after neutralising Mbe's men in the van where they monitored Chika.

As they journey home, they persistently ask Ikem to tell them what happened to him and where he's been all the while. He simply smiled and told them that there was time for the long story. Occasionally, he'd look at Udenna and they'd wink at each other.

While on the way, Chika calls the Room to inform them that everything is okay. Mbe was under arrest and all his corrupt colleagues were being fished out by the men of the FBI. Unknown to Mbe, the FBI was investigating the internal corruption that risked tearing the agency apart.

The next day, Jane, Chika and Ikem were with the team of officers that received Ejike, Ola and Kachi as they exited Room 39.

That morning, Jane was given back her father's properties that were found in his car. And among the things she found was the electronic key for the exit which Chukwuma had gone to get before he was killed. Jane hands it over to Chika.

PART FIVE

Who am I?

ROOM 39

CHAPTER 19

Today, I was at the new antiterrorism building. It's about three weeks after the whole Room 39 incident, and activities have finally resumed at the new creature of Chukwuma. This time I was there to meet with the new director, Madam Chika.

While sitting at the reception, I noticed that someone came and, without making much noise, sat beside me. Meanwhile, I was engrossed reading an interesting story on one of my favourite blogs **cabiojinia.com**. Let me quickly say that cabiojinia.com is my favourite spot for daily inspiration. It's a popular website on Pirro's lane because the writer churns out interesting articles daily. Anyway, I was reading this interesting story titled 'JIDE'S LIES,' a story I recommend everyone reads. Still engrossed in the story, I heard a voice, 'hey boy! How are you doing?'

I turned around to see if the person beside me was talking to me or maybe to someone else. When I turned, I observed that he was focused on his newspapers. So, I was a bit confused as to who spoke - my mind, himself, or a voice from my phone? I couldn't readily recognise him because he had dark shades on. I just left him and continued reading my story.

'Have you had your third shot of the vaccine yet?' The voice questioned.

At this point, I surely knew that it wasn't my mind speaking to me nor my phone playing a recorded message of some sort. *Cabiojinia.com* doesn't have audio articles, although he has promised to start a Podcast by the first quarter of 2022. So, it must be coming from the person sitting by my side.

Also, I recall that it's only one person who had asked me a similar question in the past concerning vaccination. That was several months ago while I was waiting at the DNI building on Pirro's lane. The voice is familiar, but I wasn't very sure.

'Don't be arrogant, boy! Do you have your third dose of the covid-19 vaccine or not?' The voice insisted.

This time I was sure who was talking to me. 'Well, I want to be sure that you have your Super Green Pass before I respond.' I answered.

He laughs and gently lowers his dark shades and invites me to come closer. That was the old man I met several months ago.

'How are you doing, boy?' He asked.

'I'm good, Sir. How about you?'

'Not bad. It's cool here.' He responded. I didn't quite understand what he meant by 'cool here,' but I didn't want to ask for further explanation. There was something else I wanted to hear from him.

'The last time I promised you that I'd tell you something about *if you want to travel far, travel light, right?*' He asks as if he doesn't remember his promise.

'Yes Sir, you did. And I've been dying to meet you. The ones you told me the last time were so insightful, and I've tried to live by them ever since.' I answered, excited to hear more gems from my old wise man.

'Alright. Before I tell you those, can you tell me a little bit about yourself?' He asks.

'Yes, of course.' I began by telling him my name and how I've always wanted to be a heart surgeon and a teacher of the Bible and other aspirations.

After a while, he stopped me and asked. 'What's your real name?'

I was shocked because no one has ever asked me that before. Everyone called me Cabiojinia and that's all. And quite frankly, I'm not ready to tell anyone my real name. Not even him.

'My name is Cabiojinia. My real name is Cabiojinia. It's on my ID card.' I answered.

'Youngblood, what's your real name? Not the name that everyone calls you. But the name that your parents gave you at birth.' He insists.

For a moment, I felt threatened. I felt as if all the secrets I've kept for decades were unravelled and someone was asking me for confirmation. But I refused to give in. I've worked so hard to keep my identity secret, and no one can destroy my reputation, especially now that I'm very close to my objective.

'Well, if you wouldn't tell me who you are, I won't tell you about the things you should drop if you wish to travel far.' He said.

I couldn't utter a word. I needed that counsel from him. I needed them badly. But I also want to protect Cabiojinia, a name that I've worked so hard to design and build. As I was thinking about what to do, the old man got up, picked up his staff and headed towards the door.

I quickly stood to my feet and tried pleading with him to give me a few of the things. He refused and told me that the only thing he could give me was Galatians 5:19-21.

'Read it, boy,' he said. 'If we meet again and you're willing to tell me about you, then, I'll tell you more.'

'But I need explanations for these verses.' I shouted.

'I know, but the Holy Spirit of God will help you. And if we meet again, I'll also add some words to help too. Also, next time we meet, I'll tell you another important thing: *If you don't want to travel, have all the things you need at home.*' He said as he vanished into the light that streamed into the hall from the entrance door.

As he walked away, I was happy but at the same time sad. Happy because he gave me something to hold on to, but sad because I didn't reveal my real identity to him. 'Maybe he already knows, what was the point of hiding my real name?' I pondered.

***

Okay, I'm Cabiojinia, the one telling this entire story in this book. I'm a heart surgeon working with the DNI.

But I'm also working as a covert agent for the FBI. Don't get it twisted, I'm just doing my jobs the best possible way.

Should I tell you of my relationship with Chukwuma? Because come to think of it, I'm also the journalist he was sending the secret puzzles to. Yeah, that is the covert FBI job I was doing - spying on Chukwuma... just a little.

The only mysterious person I'm yet to understand who he is and what he does is this old man that I've met twice now: first at the DNI headquarters and second here at the Antiterrorism unit. I met him the day when Ike was 'killed' and now that Ike is back to the office 'alive'. Who is he?

Well, he is my granddad. He has been my strength even when the going became very tough. He has continued to appear to me since the day I decided to uncover what happened to him.

He worked for the FBI at its formative stages before he was killed by the Collingahs. It's rumoured that some FBI agents played a vital role in his death. Since the corrupt FBI agents have been captured and jailed, the only group of people left are the Collingahs. As much as I want to follow my grandfather's counsel to drop revenge and travel light, something in me tells me that if I don't do anything, the Collingahs will continue their evil trade.

I want to obey my granddad, but I hope he understands that these evil men should proceed no further. And I hope he stays with me no matter what decision I make, even though he's only there in my imagination. Thank God I have Kachi by my side, who knows what two crazy men from distant generations can do?

And oh, one more detail I didn't tell you, I'm the fiancé of Jane, Chukwuma's daughter. I know it sounds complicated but let me explain.

I attended the same medical school as Jane. I met her during my finals; she was in her third year then. After medical school, I decided to do my residency in heart surgery at Pirro's General Hospital. During this time, we kept in contact.

While in medical school, I decided to join the military. But down the road, I switched to join the FBI and later the DNI. I know it doesn't make sense but don't judge me. I was just searching for a way to make the Collingahs pay for what they did to my granddad.

I'm also a part-time journalist with one of the local newspapers. That was a cover-up job. I wrote on health, politics, and security, but with a pseudo name Kean. So, now you know that Kean isn't my official name. Just like Cabiojinia isn't my real name, but just my blog name.

***

Wondering who called the journalist anonymously to delete the incriminating contents on his computer? Well, that was Ikem. While he was 'dead' he was working underground. He eventually discovered me and wanted some collaboration. I helped him with a few things. He's the only one that knows that I have multiple jobs, but he doesn't know my real name. He calls me Cabiojinia or Kean depending on the occasion. And that's fine by me.

My real name is Udenna, and it's only my fiancée, Jane, that knows that. But don't tell her I do these other jobs. She'll be very mad that I kept all these secrets from her for years.

Anyway, I know that some of you reading this book are spies that can't wait to reveal my identity to her. So, I've organised a dinner tonight at Chirico's restaurant at 7pm. While you'll be reading this concluding chapter, I'll be telling her all she needs to know about me including the things that will be contained in **Room 40.** And to appease her further, I shall tell her all the story in detail of my new title ''JIDE'S LIES.''

And yes, Kachi will be surprised when he finds out that I knew Jane was inside Room 39 before he ever thought of entering there. I had everything planned already from the onset.

It's alright. I'm already spoiling ROOM 40. See you in JIDE'S LIES and ROOM 40. See you at **cabiojinia.com** for more tasty stories that inspire.

God bless and keep you.

"Forgive us our debts as we forgive our debtors."
Matthew 6:12

ROOM 39

Main Characters

Kachi - Chemical engineering professor
Uyom - Kachi's wife
Nnenna - Kachi's daughter

Ejike - Mathematician and professor
Udoka - Ejike's brother

Olamma/Ola - A young architect
Ezinne - Olamma's mother
Ezenna - Olamma's father

Chukwuma - Architect
Jane - Chukwuma's daughter
Udenna - Emergency Medicine Resident, Jane's fiancé
Kean - Journalist
Old man

Chika - Director Antiterrorism unit, Ike's wife
Ike/Ikem – Senior Employee of the DNI. Chika's
husband.
Dede - Chika's father
Ebuka - Chika's son
Miss Ifunanya - Ebuka's teacher

Mbe - Corrupt FBI officer
Collingah - Drug lord

SIGN UP FOR MY NEWSLETTER

For daily inspirational articles, kindly sign up to my weekly newsletter on cabiojinia.com

There are over 300 articles on the Gospel, **Personal** Development, Leadership, Business, Education, Society & Lifestyle, Inspiring short stories, and Inspirational Nuggets.

For bookings, enquiries, corrections, collaboration, and any other good thing you wish to share with me, kindly send an email to **cabiojiniaofficial@gmail.com** or contact **+39 334 377 2769**.

Enjoy Cabiojinia, the Heart Mender.
God be with you.

About the Author

Ciao, I'm Cabiojinia.

I'm just that little boy that is chasing his dream of becoming a Cardiothoracic Surgeon. But while on that path, I inspire hundreds of people every month on my blog. I help individuals and groups discover their uniqueness and achieve their life purpose.

With articles on the Gospel, Personal Development, Leadership, Business, Education, Society & Lifestyle, Inspiring stories, and Inspirational Nuggets, I inspire you daily with something fresh and tasty.

I'm also a public speaker, a leadership coach, and a fiction writer. Currently, I'm running many series on multiple subjects on my blog, and the reviews have been quite interesting.

I'm also a passionate student of the Bible. It is my firm belief that there are uncountable mysteries (read treasures) that God hid in His Word, that if unravelled will help us lead a better life.

You'll discover that sometimes I inject a bit of Igbo language, Italian and Pidgin English in my writeups. Well, since I'm fluent in all three, why not mix them up to generate tasty stories that inspire, right?

One last thing: I'd like to introduce you to my Special Friend, Jesus, who saved me from sin and gave me the hope of eternal life. I hope you'll encounter Him and start a beautiful relationship with Him.

Printed in Great Britain
by Amazon

803653R00173